The BUSINESSMAN'S Tie

Deena Ward

The Power to Please ✌ Book One

For Hedon

Thank you ... for everything

TABLE OF CONTENTS

« CHAPTER 1 »

THE FIRST TIME I SAW him, when he looked back at me, a thrill of energy blazed through every nerve in my body. It was a tingling flash, gone in an instant, leaving me hyper-aware of his presence, and every detail I could detect across a dim, crowded room.

He stood by the bar, one arm resting on the polished surface, his shirt collar open under his jacket in a casual way, putting me in mind of a businessman relaxing on his way home from work. Was his tie in his car? I felt sure he was wearing a tie before he decided to stop for a drink.

His dark hair was brushed back from a wide and manly forehead. I couldn't tell the exact color of his eyes. Dark. I was sure his eyes were dark.

He had a fine Roman nose and a clean-shaven square jaw. Classically handsome, he would be called. He was tall, powerful-looking and muscular, though not in a bulky way. Something about him seemed familiar. Had I met him before? No. I would remember meeting this man.

There was no telling what he did for a living, but his appearance suggested a professional of some sort. I also couldn't be sure of his age, and guessed he was approaching forty.

But guessing certain details wasn't important at that time. There was only one thing I truly wanted to know.

When he looked back at me, at that first moment when our gazes met, did he experience the same jolt of connection as I?

Nothing in his demeanor suggested he felt anything at all. He simply stood there and looked back at me, not in a blank way, but in a thinking, contained way. If his nerves were jangled like mine, he didn't show it.

And then, too soon, the tingles and questions were ruined, obliterated by my friend, Sherry, who half-yelled in my ear, "See something you like?"

I blinked. Something I like? I turned to my friend. And just like that, the moment when I first saw The Businessman was over.

I played it light. "And what if I have?"

She raised her glass to me. "Good for you!" She called to our two other friends, her loud voice easily carrying over the blaring music. "Attention, ladies! Our freshly-minted divorcee here is officially ready to move on. She's spied a candidate for some single-time-to-mingle action. Raise your drinks!"

They laughed. We clinked glasses, and I played along with their ribbing since it was why we were here — to celebrate my divorce. Toast to a fresh start. Why the hell not.

They teased me about the hot men I could have with a free conscience, but I couldn't focus on what they said. They trashed my ex, declared him a loser and me a lucky lady to be through with him, my future wide open, etc., etc. Basically, it was everything we'd been saying since my husband and I split nine months earlier. The only difference now was that the split was official. I signed the papers that morning.

This chatter about my circumstances and about my ex-husband, we had hashed and rehashed so often I could have recited what everyone said before they actually said it. Normally, I enjoyed shredding my ex-husband's character, or lack thereof. But not tonight. Tonight I experienced something new. Instant attraction. With a stranger in a bar. How odd ... and thrilling.

I couldn't pay much attention to my friends because it took the majority of my mental effort to keep from searching out The Businessman, as I thought of him now, to verify he still stood by the bar. Finally, I gave in and looked his way, only a furtive glimpse so I could quickly look away should he catch me searching for him.

Ah, there he was, still standing where I last saw him, but he wasn't looking my way. He was talking to someone, an older man.

My friend Jackie poked me in the arm. "Hey! We've called your ex enough names for one night. Why don't you get on over there to Mr. Sexy and stake your claim."

I only smiled.

"I'm just saying, if you don't do it, one of these young blondies trolling around here will beat you to it."

I shrugged. "If he wants young blondes, he's welcome to them."

My friends laughed at me. They always knew when I was full of shit.

"Go on," said Sherry. "Go say hi. He won't bite."

"Or maybe he will," said Gail.

Jackie waggled an eyebrow. "I can tell he's got a taste for fresh hot divorcees on the prowl."

They continued in this fashion, fully enjoying themselves, until I couldn't take it anymore and escaped with the classic line of "I've got to use the restroom."

They didn't buy it, but the restroom excuse is sacred, and there was nothing they could do but heckle my back as I fled into the crowd.

I had to walk by The Businessman to reach the restroom and I couldn't resist, on my way, trying to catch his eye. He did glance my way as I passed, but not at my face. He gave my body a quick and intimate once-over. Feet to chest, and there he stopped.

I should have been insulted, but I wasn't. Maybe it was because I'd had three stiff drinks. Most likely, it was because I hoped he liked what he saw. If he'd been some smelly jerk lingering on a street corner, my reaction would have been a biting, vocal opposite.

By the time I reached the hallway that led to the bathrooms, my face was hot from embarrassment. I spent several minutes in the ladies room, standing at the lavatory getting myself together, reminding myself what I was doing. I was having fun, that was all. I remembered how to have fun, didn't I? Oh, hell, who knew.

Did I ever have fun, even before my marriage? Regardless, now was the time to start.

I told myself that, as soon as I left the restroom, I would introduce myself to The Businessman. I would do it. I would. Go girl.

I checked myself one last time in the mirror before I charged into my mission. Look out, sexy stranger, I thought. Here comes a woman with a plan. I pulled the door open.

But I didn't get the chance to put that plan into action.

The Businessman stood in the hallway.

He leaned against the paneled wall, his arms crossed casually. Up close like this, he was taller than I thought he'd be. He was powerfully built, solid under his suit jacket and open-collared shirt. He had sexy, half-lidded eyes as he gave me another once over, then met my gaze.

That strange energy thrummed through me, similar to the one before. My brain seemed to stop working, as if I could only experience the world through this sensation, this sensual connection that coiled between me and The Businessman.

No, that's not right. To be fair, my brain still worked. I simply ignored it. My brain told me to get the hell out of the hall. It warned that I wasn't ready for whatever this stranger offered, or for what he might take. It ordered me to run away from the dangerous character. Forget about fun. Think about what you're doing.

My tingling body, however, told me I shouldn't jump to conclusions. Let the moment play out. Forget about caution and explore the possibilities. I was free and pushing 30, and I didn't need anyone else's permission to do what I wanted. This man was without doubt the most magnetic, sexy man I'd ever seen. And if I weren't mistaken, he was interested in me, too.

With three drinks of buzzed confidence and freshly-signed divorce papers whispering permission, my body made a far more appealing argument than my brain.

Then The Businessman smiled a small, knowing smile. His half-grin was an invitation. It said, come on, do you dare?

It was as if a haze rose in the hallway, and the only thing I could see clearly was the powerful man with the wicked smile. My awareness of him was acute, intense. Something about him. Something.

I knew I wanted him. I wanted to kiss that grin and taste exactly what it was he offered, what he might take.

When he held out a hand to me, I stepped forward and grasped it, and he led me past the ladies room, farther down the hall, into a darkened corridor which branched to the right off the main hall. I could make out a closed door at the end of the corridor, but couldn't see clearly with the only lighting coming indirectly from the main hall. We stopped about halfway to the closed door.

Had I gone insane? What was I doing? We hadn't even spoken to one another and here I was following him into the shadows of a noisy old bar. But I wasn't much attending any of the thoughts that I should have been attending. My body had triumphed over my brain, and I wasn't heeding reason. My senses were focused on the man holding my hand. Even the loud music from the bar faded into the distance.

Anyone walking to the end of the main hallway could have seen us back there, a pair of dark silhouettes moving in the shadows. The Businessman pulled me to him, held my face and leaned down to kiss me. His lips barely touched mine. It seemed he was breathing me in and I did the same.

We brushed lips and he tasted of clean freshness and of the bourbon he'd been drinking. I smelled the spicy scent of his cologne and I laid my hands against his hard chest. His masculine fragrance mingled with the other smells in the corridor, grainy spilled beer and the tang of pine paneling, the bite of the dust we stirred up from the old carpeting.

Our kiss slowly grew more intense. I opened my mouth and he entered it with a hard tongue. One of his arms slipped around my waist, behind my back, pulling me closer while I raised my arms to his shoulders and wrapped them around his neck.

This kissing was a feral thing, out of control. On my part, at least. For The Businessman, I thought not.

I didn't question anything. I didn't worry about people walking down the main hallway and seeing me. I didn't fret over being alone, necking with a stranger. I was of the moment and my body felt alive in a way it never had. My heart raced as he kissed me in what felt increasingly like a claim. We weren't kissing each other. He was claiming me.

His mouth moved over mine with smooth and firm expertise. He held my face and took what he wanted, leaving me breathless and ready for more.

I don't know how long we did this. I was lost. And so when everything changed, it took me a while to catch up.

We'd been kissing, so close and tight together, my breasts mashed against his hard chest, my fingers groping at the sinewy toughness of his back. And then it all changed.

In a swift and smooth movement, he pushed away from me, seized my hands and raised them over my head. In another movement, he turned me around and shoved me into the wall, front-first, my hot cheek pressed against the cool paneling.

It seemed only a microsecond passed until he smashed his body against the back of mine to hold me still, while at the same time he secured my hands to a fixture on the wall, above my head.

Just like that, I was bound ... and nearly helpless. I felt his warm breath on my ear. I wasn't sure what had happened. I twisted and bent my head back far enough to see my restraints. There it was, wrapped around my wrists. The Businessman's tie.

I stupidly thought, "So that's what he did with it."

My reaction after that, though, was instinctual. I pulled. I pulled, and my breath which was already shortened from The Businessman's kisses became rough and ragged from a ripening panic. I didn't want to be helpless. I had to get away. I may have said no. I don't know why I didn't yell, but I'm certain I didn't.

I didn't want to be tied up by a stranger. I pulled harder but was unable to gain purchase because of his hard weight pressed against my back. My panic increased.

Before it went full-blown, The Businessman spoke his first words to me.

His voice was deep and soothing. "I'll let you go if that's what you want."

I slowed my frantic pulling. He ... would let me go ... if I want? I made a few more weak pulls as I considered what he said. What was this? A trick?

He trailed his fingertips down the sides of my raised arms, so very, very slowly, raising goosebumps as he went. Then he continued down both sides of my body, past my breasts, down my waist and hips, and onward to my upper legs. And there he stopped, toying with the bare flesh of my thighs, millimeters below the hem of my skirt.

"I'll let you go, if you want," he said.

I shuddered lightly.

His words fell on my sensitive skin in a heated tickle. "But I don't think that's what you want."

I shuddered again as his fingertips played up and under the bottom of my skirt, climbing higher, my nerves dancing under his touch.

I stopped trying to free myself. My breath slowed as if I were holding it in anticipation of where his fingers might travel next. My panic morphed into desire, wanting him to touch more.

He took a half-step back to give himself room to explore. When his fingertips of fire reached the bottom curve of my buttocks, and my breath audibly caught in my throat, he stopped moving, leaned over so I could see into his dark eyes. "Are you afraid of me?"

I swallowed the lump his words raised in my throat, and answered with a weakness I didn't expect. "Yes ... no."

"Good. Do you want me to let you go?"

I shook my head.

"Say the words," he said.

I knew I would say the words. I knew I would say just about anything he wanted me to say, with his fingers lightly touching the bottom of my ass, right at the edge of my panties and on the verge of heading I hoped I knew where.

"I don't want you to let me go," I said.

"Good." His only response.

He leaned back again, and I was jerked roughly when he grabbed my panties and yanked them down my legs. I thought I heard them tear, and I gasped then gritted my teeth at the momentary pain caused by the elastic biting into my skin. He lifted my feet, one at a time, then sent my panties sailing away somewhere down the dark hall.

He rolled up the back of my skirt and tucked it into the waistband, baring my ass. My face grew warm when he did nothing for a few moments. I assumed he was standing there looking at me. I tried not to think about it. And I tried not to imagine someone else seeing me from the hall. But mostly, I tried not to admit how both those thoughts excited me far more than they frightened me.

"Arch your back and stick out your ass," he said.

I didn't act quickly enough, apparently, since he pushed a hand into the small of my back, and with the other hand roughly reached between my legs and pulled backwards.

While I tried to adjust to the feel of him on my most private parts, he continued to give me orders. "Hold it like that. Spread your legs. Wider. Don't move."

And then his hands were gone again. "Pretty," he said, then nothing more.

My face must have been scarlet by then. I was on display to this stranger, and really, to anyone who might wander down the main hall and glance our way. What if someone were standing over there at this moment, right now, watching the tall, powerful man arrange me for his viewing pleasure?

I pictured the scene in my head, as if I stood in that hallway, watching a different me, tied and helpless, back arched, ass thrust out, exposed, a fully-clothed stranger scrutinizing, exploring. It was humiliating and thrilling. I was on fire.

God, I wanted his hands on me. Please bring them back.

As if he heard, The Businessman reached between my legs and trailed his fingers all the way from my clitoris to my ass. His fingers were slick as they slid, slick from me.

I shuddered and it wasn't difficult to hold the pose he placed me in. I pushed my butt out as far as I could. To find him.

He toyed with me a few seconds more, stroking up and down, down and up. Then with both hands, he took hold of my labia and pulled them apart. He held me open for a while, as if this, also, he must inspect, though surely it was too dark for him to see much. He squeezed and pulled on my flesh with demanding fingers, mixing the thrill from this unexpected action with the discomfort of his pinches.

Hold and pull. Pinch and pull. Watching. Watching. He watched this most intimate part of me as he played.

And then he let go and shoved two fingers inside me. I groaned. Oh, God. I groaned loudly. I was ready for the invasion, and his fingers entered me easily, though they felt large at the same time, stretching me. It felt like heaven. I tingled practically everywhere.

How long had it been since anyone was inside me? I couldn't remember. It didn't matter. Not now.

He slid his fingers in and out. Slowly, he increased the force until he was pumping his fingers into me. Pumping, pumping. Deliberately and forcefully, he pounded his fingers into my pussy. Those fingers felt so large and long, and I pushed against him.

Straining to get closer, I ground myself into his fist as he finger-fucked me. He drove inside me ever harder, pounding me, really, the force of impact an ever-spreading spike of pain. I stopped straining toward him. And yet the pleasure, God, the pleasure. It grew too.

Pounding me, pounding me. I tried to shrink away. A deliberate thrust. Rhythmic. Harder, ever harder. Pleasure. Pain. I wanted it. I didn't want it. His fingers inside me. Then gone. Then ramming home. Forceful. Distinct. I grunted. Mmph. Pound. Mmph. Pound.

Finally, I shrank away from him so far that I pressed flush against the wall, my cheek once more mashed against the paneling. But the pounding didn't stop. Mmph! Pound. And then I couldn't stop myself — I tried to close my legs around his hand.

A big mistake on my part, I quickly discovered.

The Businessman immediately stopped. Just like that. He made a clipped sound of disgust and like a flash of lightening, he smacked my ass three times. Smack! Smack! Smack! Hard as hell. Not playful. Not fun. Hard as hell. And it hurt like hell, too. I cried out. What was this?

His voice was low, but clearly audible over the distant noises from the bar. "Resume the pose."

I was confused and befuddled from desire and heat and pain. I wasn't allowed any time to consider my options, to even realize I had options.

Smack! Smack! Smack! He struck my ass again. I cried out once more and yanked on the restraining tie.

"Stop," he said.

And oddly enough, I did.

"Either you resume the pose," he said, "or I'll stop doing this." He slid his hand between my closed legs and slipped his fingers inside me. He began some kind of twisting dance in there and made me groan.

"Decide now, or we're done," he said.

His fingers were magical things, making me not care about the pain of the spanking, or anything really, except that he not stop. It became clear what I needed to do, and I could only wonder that I had ever been confused.

So I resumed the pose, of course.

He'd get whatever he wanted, as long as he didn't stop.

He twisted his fingers around inside me, making me squirm. With his other hand, he rubbed my ass cheeks, soothing the fiery residuals of his swats. I moaned.

The rising heat from the spanking and his rubbing added to the sensuality of his motions. What was he doing, anyway? I'd never felt anything like it. I moved my hips in rhythm with his clever fingers, a need building inside me for more, more. Something more.

My pussy still ached from his pounding, and my ass still burned from his spanking, but those fingers of his ... oh well, those fingers working and working. Mmm. There was no getting enough. I closed my eyes and floated on it.

His voice filtered through to me, seemingly from a distance. "You have a beautiful ass. I would imagine anyone walking down that hall over there would love to see it. Don't you think?"

I groaned. Oh God. A reminder of the hall. My naked ass and pussy. Anyone could see. But more than that, he saw me. I didn't know. I couldn't think.

"Shall I fuck you now?" he asked.

This, I did know. I panted and answered with a breathy, "Yes."

"Yes what?"

I opened my eyes. "Yes I want you to fuck me." Shameless in my need.

He stopped moving his fingers, though he left them inside me. Then he stopped rubbing my ass. I held my breath. Now he would pull out his dick and thrust it inside me. That's what I wanted. I needed him to fill me as only his cock could.

He leaned forward and delivered an ominous whisper. "You might be a very foolish young woman."

I couldn't give his statement much thought, though I had no doubt he was right. I had no doubt he was right about anything and everything, as long as his fingers started moving again, or he fucked me. Whatever. Was that foolish?

"You stepped into a dark hall with a stranger," he continued, "in a noisy bar where it's unlikely anyone would hear your screams."

I nodded. No doubt about it. He was right on that one. It was pretty damned stupid of me. But I couldn't be bothered by it for long, not when his other hand slipped around my hip and found its way to my clit. He rubbed it gently. Oh God. Tingles and heat. A pang low in my belly. A rising pressure.

He shifted so I could see his face, see into his dark, dark eyes. "But I'm going to give you the benefit of the doubt tonight," he said, "and assume this isn't something you'd normally do."

His fingers twitched inside me again. Clearly and distinctly, as if he wanted to make sure I registered each and every word, he said, "I'm going to believe that you saw what I did."

I moaned and pushed against him, rolling my hips. I wasn't certain what he meant. The world had turned into a wonderland of pure sensation. His fingers. Magical fingers. And when would he fuck me? I didn't want him to stop what he was doing, but at the same time, I was ready for him. I wanted it.

"Please fuck me," I said. The blatant, pleading words would surprise me when I remembered them later.

His dark eyes narrowed as he looked at me, then he smiled. "You don't get what you want. I get what I want."

And with that, he pulled out of me and began to spank me, this time on my pussy. Smack! A sharp fiery strike. If I tried to pull away, he forced me back and smacked harder. Smack! On my ass. I fought my instinct to escape, and struggled to hold the pose he wanted.

Then his fingers were inside me again. And he returned to rubbing my clit in the most delicious way, circling around and around. And his fingers inside me, they resumed their special dance.

He did none of this quickly, or in a rushed frenzy. Far from it. Each action was measured, considered. Even when it changed, it was done in a conscious way. He pulled his fingers out of me and slapped my pussy. Then he shoved his fingers into me again. Pound. Pound. Pound. Was he twisting his hand? A deliberate one, two, three. Then a withdrawal, and a fierce blow to my pussy or my ass.

Pound. The staccato burst of a stinging slap. And all the while he teased my clit with feathery circles and flicks. I could have come at any moment.

The sensations nearly peaked in my belly, the tightness ready for release, but each time I came close, he changed the rhythm or the pressure, or whatever it was he was doing, and my imminent need to come decreased. Then he began building me up again.

Each smack of my pussy and ass was distinct. Each thrust inside done with controlled fierceness. I experienced each act individually, even as they bled into the whole.

He smacked and pounded me until tears ran down my cheeks and I gasped for air. Fingers in me. Fingers out. Pinches. Flicks. Spanks. I wanted to get away but there was no way I could or would. I craved the release. Couldn't do without it. He drove me to the point that I rose to meet him as he shoved into me.

Please, please. I may have even said the words. And then ...

I came. I came hard and total. My body rocked from it, shuddering as the orgasm rolled through me.

The Businessman found some spot inside me and rubbed it hard as I came. I went to a higher level. The climax was shattering and lasted longer than I thought possible. The bliss of it. God. It was nearly too much, nearly more than I knew how to deal with. Nearly.

As my orgasm died away, The Businessman removed his fingers and cupped my pussy in his hand, holding me, most likely feeling the receding twitches of my clit and pussy as my climax subsided. A pulse. And then another. Then longer until the next.

When it passed at last, The Businessman let go of me, and I slumped against the wall. I no longer gasped for air, but I still breathed hard and my heartbeat had yet to return to normal. From time to time, bursts of aftershocks skittered over my body, leaving goosebumps in their wake.

I was only vaguely aware of The Businessman righting my skirt. It fell against the back of my thighs. My legs felt shaky and quivery.

He reached out and grabbed the hair at the base of my head and tilted me back enough to see him looming over me.

"Who are you?" I asked, my voice a stunted whisper.

"You know who I am, and I know you. We knew the instant our eyes met," he said.

I knew that he was right in one respect, that I felt something powerful when I saw him. I didn't know what it was, what to call it, other than desire. Was it something else, something more? What did he mean when he said I knew him? Desire wasn't knowledge, was it? I gulped hard.

His eyes were intense and black and he spoke in a way that was almost sinister. "Our kind will always find one another."

The way he said it. The fierce look, the stern line of his lips. The power.

I thought, now he will take me, and I will fly apart in the dark hall of this noisy bar. He'll throw me on the dirty floor, and I won't care. In fact, I'll like that it's filthy.

He'll take me from behind and shove his cock into me and fuck me until I beg for mercy. And I ... will fly ... apart.

Except none of that happened. He didn't take me.

The intensity left his face as if it had never been there. Had I only imagined it? No, I hadn't imagined it, but it was gone nonetheless, replaced by a smooth calmness. He gave me an enigmatic smile.

He untied my hands, smoothed out my clothes and pushed my hair into half-assed order. He picked up my purse and stuck it under my arm.

Holding my hand, he led me back to the main hallway then to the door of the ladies room. I followed along like some silly, brainless thing.

"You should clean yourself up," he said. "Your girlfriends will be getting worried about you."

He leaned down and gave me an oddly chaste kiss.

"It was a pleasure," he said, then he opened the door of the restroom and gently nudged me inside. The door closed and he was gone.

I was alone.

I thought, "My name is Nonnie Crawford. And yours?"

« CHAPTER 2 »

I SAT IN A STALL in the restroom, trying to pull myself into some sort of order. I wondered how long we'd been in that shadowy corridor. I couldn't be certain of duration, but surely it was long enough for my friends to get worried about me.

Where were they, anyway? I could have been robbed and stabbed, or dragged off through the back door, raped and killed in the back lot, my body left lifeless and crumpled next to a reeking dumpster.

When I went to a bar with friends, I expected them to look after me. They should have been tearing around the place, calling my name, frantic and insistent that I be found. So where were they? I wanted to stalk up to our table and chew them out for putting me in danger.

I stood up to go do just that ... but I stopped, and sat back down. I wasn't really angry at my friends. I was angry at myself. They hadn't put me in danger; I managed that all on my own. Stupid, stupid, stupid. What was I thinking?

I hadn't been thinking. I'd been acting on some bizarre compulsion. It was an anomaly, an erotically-fueled error of judgment. Luckily I survived no worse for the wear, the only repercussions being a sore bottom, and the loss of a pair of panties.

I groaned. God, I had no panties. I wanted to go home and climb into my bed and sleep the sleep of the stupid and wicked for a week.

I sighed and slogged to the mirror. I expected to see a smeared and smudged Smoking Gun mugshot looking back at me. But no, it wasn't too bad. Tear tracks on my cheeks were the most obvious evidence of my encounter, nothing a little water and some mascara and lipstick couldn't fix. By the time I completed my repairs, the only reminder on my face was the heightened color of my cheeks.

I was thoroughly aware of my underwear problem when I exited the restroom, and couldn't resist holding one of my hands against the side of my skirt. Just in case, I thought. It was nothing more than a gesture, but I needed the reassurance.

I didn't look at The Businessman as I passed by him, though I noticed from the corner of my eye that he'd resumed his former position and chatted with the same man as before. I kept my gaze directed forward, seeking out the safety of the table where I'd left my friends.

As soon as I saw them, I knew why they hadn't come to find me — two men had joined our table. Of course. They probably had no idea how long I'd been gone. Too busy flirting.

I sat down to a flurry of introductions and smiles and comments of how they were starting to worry about me and was I okay and so on and so forth. I gave all the appropriate fibbing answers.

The two men had a couple more friends who joined us, managed to squeeze in around the table, bringing more drinks for the group. Oh boy. This was too much. I accepted the drink, though. I needed it.

I played the game as best I could and hoped to cover my distraction. I snuck an occasional glance toward The Businessman, but never caught his eye.

It struck me as bizarre that I knew the name of the man sitting next to me, Kevin, but that I didn't know the name of the man who had ripped my panties and done things to me that made sitting in my chair more than a bit uncomfortable. Why hadn't he told me his name? Rude. Disdainful. As if I weren't worthy of knowing it. As if my name weren't worth being known.

I considered going to him and demanding he tell me his name. And then I would tell him mine. I almost worked up the courage when I looked his way again and saw he was gone. I scanned the bar. He wasn't there. Wait. There he was, leaving with his friend. I could still catch him, I thought, as the door closed behind him. But I didn't.

I stayed put and half-listened to Kevin drone about a concert he'd attended.

Perhaps it was best that The Businessman go.

The remainder of the evening dragged until I had to plead a headache to get my friends to take me home. They were jolly on the drive, having met new men, exchanged phone numbers and done all the things they hoped to do at the beginning of the evening; in other words, they garnered dates to fill future Friday nights.

I made it into my apartment without suffering a skirt catastrophe. I showered then pulled on a t-shirt and climbed into bed. I was asleep within moments.

I slept hard, dreamless, until nearly noon the next day, which thankfully was Saturday. When I first woke up, I didn't think about what I'd done the night before. I just did what I normally did in the mornings, a routine which began with coffee.

I didn't think about anything until I sat down at the kitchen table to drink my coffee. Ouch. I squirmed on the chair. Still a bit sore. From ... oh yeah, that's right. I was still sore from letting a stranger have his way with me in a dirty back hallway. I closed my eyes and groaned. Ugh.

The rest of my day proceeded in pretty much the same fashion. I would keep myself busy and sidetracked and then I would remember and begin the self-chastisement, and then I would do something so I'd forget, and repeat, and repeat.

I had no plans for the evening apart from watching a movie I rented earlier in the week. While watching the movie, memories of what happened in that corridor kept popping into my head. Eventually, I gave up and turned off the television. I sat there, thinking.

I am a powerful woman. I left my husband mostly because he was weak and I couldn't afford that weakness in my life anymore. I determined that I didn't owe him anything, that it wasn't my mission in life to prop him up and do for him what he was too weak-willed to do for himself.

For more than ten years I had propped up the dead love of a pair of high school sweethearts who had foolishly married right after graduation. I'd acted as the sturdy support while he was the dreamer. He dreamed and I worked. I studied and barely made it through college, while he dreamed some more. I found a new job that paid our bills, while his dreams faded and I encouraged him to keep them alive.

I remembered days without end of him lying on the couch. Had he been drinking? Probably. It didn't matter, really. It didn't sustain him.

I sustained him. He drank my power as if he deserved it, as if I owed it to him. He took it and left me with nothing for myself. When I truly understood this, I left him. And we were broken apart forever.

I wanted more for myself. I wanted everything.

Last night, only a few hours after the declaration of my freedom became official, I was supposed to begin a new life where I claimed myself for myself. My power belonged to me and I would give it away to no one.

And then, I met the eyes of a stranger. I looked at him and with no thought at all, I allowed him to diddle me in a dirty hallway. He used me, pawed me, fingered me, then left me without telling me his name. Without asking for mine. He seized my power with appalling ease, my power to say no, to tell him that wasn't who I was.

I wasn't some easy slut who allowed anyone with a penis to do as they pleased with her body. But The Businessman did as he pleased. And I let him. It was raunchy and filthy and ...

It was the most erotic encounter of my life.

I sat perfectly still. There was the truth. It was the most erotic moment of my life.

For all the wrong I'd done the night before, there was a right-ness there, too. The clench in my belly when he posed me for his enjoyment. The fear and anticipation of a witness peeking from the main hall. The biting restraint of his tie around my wrists. The sting of a slap. His hands sliding over me, inside me.

My breasts began to tingle and I sighed when I thought of how he'd never touched my breasts. I longed for his touch.

That wasn't wrong. It couldn't be wrong.

I could continue berating myself, or I could just own what I'd done. I could take the tryst in the hallway as a coming out, a glimpse at what I was capable of feeling. I hadn't known a real orgasm until The Businessman shattered me into pieces. It was luck, maybe fate, that I should learn this new thing on the night of my debut.

My time in that shadowy corridor was up. Over and done with. No more worries and definitely no more guilt. I owned my sexuality. It belonged to me, and it was separate from what I'd believed about right and wrong. It simply was.

That night, I dreamed of The Businessman.

« CHAPTER 3 »

"I'll let you go if that's what you want."

While I was at work, while I was shopping, while I had a drink with a friend, while I drove, and especially when I was slept, I would hear him, his deep voice in my ear, the warmth of his breath falling on my skin, his hard chest an iron shield against my back.

"I'll let you go if that's what you want."

And I'd be in that hall again, with him, remembering how his fingertips grazed the sensitive skin on the undersides of my arms. Or remembering his hands slipping beneath the edges of my panties. The smack of his palm on my ass.

It's a good thing I'm not a surgeon or an air traffic controller. As an office manager for a mid-sized cosmetics company, my distractions over the next week didn't cause any horrific accidents of a lasting kind. Okay, so I forgot to tell our western regional sales team that we'd be meeting on Thursday instead of Wednesday. Could have been worse. I could have amputated a wrong leg or sent a plane hurtling into the river. A disgruntled sales crew was nothing in comparison.

All the same, I took my job seriously, and tried hard to focus on the tasks at hand. I tried to push away the memories. Get on with things. Forget.

By the time Saturday rolled back around, I was forced to admit I'd made no headway in forgetting my encounter with The Businessman. Kevin, the other man I met that night, had called and asked me out on a date, but I told him no. I couldn't think of anyone but The Businessman.

I relived my tryst with him countless times. I dared to fantasize about a second encounter. I kept thinking about how we hadn't even actually had sex. He was a man. He would want sex, right? All men wanted sex.

Not that it mattered whether he did or didn't want to fuck. I didn't know his name, let alone his phone number.

To keep myself busy I decided to clean out my closet and organize the shelves. When I found the purse I had carried to the bar the week before, I opened it to clean out the few cosmetics I hadn't bothered to put away that night. I pulled out a lipstick and some mascara and a pen and back in the corner a ... what was this? My hand closed around a silky fabric. I pulled it out.

It was The Businessman's tie.

Really.

I stood there and stared at it like it was some foreign thing, as if I didn't know the thing hanging from my fingers, a specimen of unknown origin.

But of course, I knew its origin. It belonged to The Businessman. He must have put it in my purse before he returned it to me.

I studied this physical evidence of Eros. The tie was a dark blue silk, with a deeper shade in diagonal stripes. It felt slinky and cool in my hand. I checked the label. Some Italian name I wasn't familiar with, but that wasn't surprising since my husband never had a reason to wear ties when he was wallowing on the couch.

There was nothing on the tie to indicate the name of the owner. Damn.

So why had he given it to me?

Perhaps it was meant to be a memento, a little something for me to remember him by. Or perhaps it was a calling card that he left for all the women from his hallway dalliances, an accessorized version of a slashed "Z" for Zorro. If so, his conceit verged on the ridiculous.

No, I couldn't believe that was it. I didn't know who this man was, but I couldn't believe him ridiculous.

In the mindless way we do things sometimes, I raised the tie to my nose and inhaled. It smelled like him, spicy, masculine and clean. I sensed him in that scent, surrounding and looming over me in the shadows. His voice, a deep rumble coming from behind.

I remembered something he said.

"Our kind will always find one another."

I thought he would take me when he said it. But he didn't. And I didn't understand why not. The intensity in his eyes, in his voice, as if he meant more than he was saying, I interpreted it as a command to remember his words. Even then. More so now.

And then I suddenly understood what he meant. I realized why he left his tie in my purse.

He wanted me to find him.

I held the tie to my nose again and breathed in his scent. It was like a time machine delivering me back to the minutes I spent with him. I still wasn't sure what he meant when he had said "our kind," but I was certain he wanted me to find him.

Funny how an entire week of trying to forget him was immediately trumped by one millisecond of a hint that he wanted to be with me. If I'd known his name and number, I would have called him right away.

The only thing I could think to do was return to the bar and see if he were there. Lots of people have favorite hangouts and maybe that bar was his. I had no other clues and if he truly wanted to see me again, he had to know my only lead was the bar.

It was still early enough in the evening that I had plenty of time to primp myself to within an inch of my life. Silly, I thought, but did it anyway. Hair shining and hanging loose down my back (all the better for him to grab it), minimal makeup (no one looks good in raccoon eyes), sexy lacy bra and panties (not my most expensive, should they be torn and tossed again, and please let them be torn and tossed again), a silky blouse, a skirt and a decent pair of heels. This was the best I had to offer. It would have to do.

The bar was mostly full when I arrived, but I found a barstool to perch on that enjoyed a decent view of the room. I scanned every nook and cranny of the place while I waited for the bartender to fill my drink order.

The Businessman wasn't there. I tried not to be disappointed. Whenever I thought of seeing him again, a flutter passed low through my belly. What would I say when I saw him? What if I was wrong about him wanting me to find him? Hell.

An hour later he still wasn't there, though I'd fended off a handful of soused potential suitors looking to provide me with drinks and a quick roll in the hay. They kept filling the empty seat beside me. Bothersome. I was relieved when, after I barely fended off a drunk and rowdy car salesman, a young woman sat next to me.

She smiled at me and I smiled back. She was in her early twenties, a lovely thing, small and dainty, with long blonde hair and a pixie-like face. She wore a pink slip of a dress that showed off her lithe figure. I might have been a little jealous if it hadn't been for her easy smile and welcoming manner.

She said her name was Lilly and that she'd been waiting on a date in the restaurant next door but that he stood her up. I couldn't imagine what kind of jackass would stand up this little jewel of a woman, and I said something along those lines. She laughed.

We chatted for a while about men being scumbags, etc., the things we women say when we believe we've been rejected. Lilly was a pleasant companion and kept the drunks at bay with minimal fuss. She wielded an excellent derisive stare that sent them scrambling away within seconds. I nearly laughed out loud the first time I saw her effortlessly send an impostor whimpering away in disgrace.

All the while, I never quit scanning the room, seeking out my dark-haired stranger. All to no avail.

After several drinks, Lilly became more and more talkative. She told me about a nightclub she once visited with the man who stood her up that very evening.

She spoke in a lowered voice as if she were telling a secret. "It was a really crazy place. All sorts of things were going on."

"What kind of things?"

"You know." She made a funny face. "Sex things."

"Really? Sex things? Like ..."

"I think it was a sex club. You've heard of those, right? People go there to hook up and have sex."

"No. Those places aren't real ... are they?"

"I think they are. And I think some kinky stuff was going down in the back rooms of this club." Her expression filled with comical intrigue.

"Hmm," was all I could think to say.

"I didn't actually see anything, though," she continued. "I just suspect it because of what some of the people were wearing."

"Such as?"

"You know, leather, corsets, that sort of thing."

"Maybe it was a Goth bar."

"I don't think so," she murmured, and looked down at her drink. "I've been thinking about that place a lot, and I'd kind of like to go back, you know, to see if I'm right."

Well I'll be damned, I thought to myself. Lilly didn't look like the kinky type. But who knew. I didn't think I was the kinky type either until I met The Businessman.

"Listen," Lilly said. "You seem like a nice girl and I like you even though I just met you. I don't have any friends that I can ask to go with me to that nightclub. Do you think you might ..." Her voice trailed away and she gave me a little, hopeful smile.

"Do you want me to go with you to a sex club?"

"I don't know for sure that it's a sex club. I don't want to get your hopes up or anything." She laughed then said, "Really, though, maybe you're right and it's just a Goth hangout. But it might be fun to check it out, and it's not like there's anything happening here."

I couldn't argue with her about that. It was nearly 10:30 and I hadn't seen a trace of The Businessman. Maybe he only came on Fridays.

I went out that evening seeking a tryst with a dark, handsome stranger. I didn't find him. Maybe the next logical step was a trip to a sex club. Ha! Liar, liar. I wanted to see the sex club, if that's what it was.

Lilly's eager smile and cute pixie face sealed the deal for me.

"Okay," I said. "What the hell." At least it would take my mind off of how to find The Businessman, and it could make a good story the next time I talked to my girlfriends.

We paid our tabs and lucked into getting a cab quickly. Less than twenty minutes later we stood outside the alleged sex club.

Cars lined the sidewalks on either side of the street. In front of us stood a huge brick building that ran nearly the entire length of the block, the building's many tall windows stretching in a regular line down the wall. All the windows were blacked out. The place looked like an old factory from the 1900s.

Most likely, it housed multiple businesses, or maybe loft apartments, though all I could see was a single black door with a lone light hanging over it. On the door a small sign read, "Private Residence." Nothing indicated this was anything resembling a night club.

I gave Lilly a questioning look. "Are you sure this is the place?"

"Definitely. Did you expect it to say 'Sex Club?'"

I laughed. I didn't have any idea what to expect.

She took my hand and pulled me to the door. "I think it's supposed to be a joke, the name, you know. Come on."

She opened the door and we entered a small, well-lit foyer. The lack of exterior signs was more than compensated for with a jumble of signs lining the walls of the foyer. I had no time to study them, but mostly they were about being 21 years old and the usual sort of warnings clubs post. I think one sign had a list of rules, but I didn't get the chance to read it.

A muscular man, clearly of the bouncer variety, lounged on a stool near another closed black door at the rear of the foyer. Now that I was inside, I heard strains of music coming from beyond the door, particularly the thumping bass.

"Good evening, ladies," said the man. "Just the two of you tonight?"

Lilly beamed her pixie smile. "That's right."

He waved toward the door. "Go ahead," he said, then went back to reading his weightlifting magazine.

We went through the door and into another short foyer, this time dimly lit. Probably it was designed to prevent the strong light in the entrance from spoiling the lighting inside the club. Sure enough, the next door opened into the club itself.

It was large. And loud, with a good-sized crowd. Basically, it looked like any run-of-the-mill dance club. Lights flashed and music pulsed. There was a long shiny bar that ran the length of one side of the room. A large dance floor was ringed with tables and chairs. High-backed round booths settled against the remaining walls. Stairs led to a second story which was a balcony overlooking the dance floor.

It smelled like beer and whiskey, of money being handled by sweaty hands, the overbearing combination of too many heavy-handed sprays of perfume, the musk of the sexual hunt.

In other words, it looked and smelled like any average night club, except for one thing — the people.

Many of them were dressed exactly as expected, decked out in their sexiest clothes for a night of partying. But in among these regular types were others who, as Lilly promised, were decked out in some wild leather garb. Snug, studded leather pants. Corsets cinched so tightly I couldn't imagine how the women, and a few men, managed to breathe. Shorty crop tops allowed glimpses of the undersides of breasts. Latex dresses. Crazy high stiletto heels. Thigh-high shiny black boots. Some people had multiple piercings and wore thick collars around their necks.

And still, this could have been a Goth thing, except that I spotted a woman in the crowd, dressed in a corset, black panties, some kind of webbed stockings ... I could have sworn I saw her moseying through the crowd leading a shirtless man by a leash that was hooked to what appeared to be nipple rings.

I wasn't a prude, or some innocent young thing with no experience in the big bad world. However, I'd never seen a man being led around on a leash ... other than on HBO. A leash attached to nipple rings. That was some serious motivation not to lag behind your leader.

Lilly pulled me farther into the club and toward an empty booth. It was set apart from the dance floor and the speakers, and so was a bit quieter, allowing you to be heard without yelling.

We ordered more drinks even though I didn't think I needed another one. We spent our time nursing our cocktails while Lilly giggled over the sight of several bar patrons with particularly outrageous garb.

Eventually, she pointed out an area in the back of the room which appeared to be a hallway. A sign over the entry proclaimed "VIP. No entry without invitation."

"I think there are rooms back there where you know, they do stuff." Her voice was too loud, I thought. She was getting tipsy.

A VIP area. Good grief. Lots of clubs had that. It was nothing more than a scam to trick shallow suckers into overpaying for booze. A VIP area was no proof that this was a sex club. How disappointing.

Now that the first excitement of possibility had worn off, I noticed that we weren't the only people who were staring. We, in fact, were being stared at by the other club patrons. Some of them simply glanced our way then moved on. Some were rude and let their gazes linger on Lilly and me. I couldn't tell exactly what their expressions were saying, but it was either "who the hell are these women trespassing on our turf," or "yum, fresh meat." Hard to say which.

Lilly appeared to notice none of this. She chattered away about this and that, and how ooh, don't you think those heels would give you bunions and so on. I half-listened.

Some of the looks we received were starting to unnerve me, and I began a plan to escape, either with or without Lilly, should it become necessary. Fresh meat. That couldn't be what those people were thinking. But if they were ... I shouldn't have been feeling anticipation. A growing excitement. A desire to flee. A greater desire to stay.

The colored strobes of the moving spotlights and the thumping underbeats of the dance music acted on my senses, making me feel connected to the pace of the club. And sexy. Connected and sexy. What the hell. Of course that's how I felt. These places were designed to seduce, to make you want to dance and flirt and rub against someone.

I realized I'd had one cocktail too many.

A tall man approached our table. I elbowed Lilly and told her to shoot him her best fuck-off stare. She began to do just that, but when she looked over at him, she stopped, her expression a blank still life. An instant of something else replaced the blankness, awareness perhaps, or fear. No, not fear. What was it? Regardless, she didn't give him her fuck-off stare so he strolled up to our table.

Once I got a closer look at him, I was glad she hadn't run him off. He was good-looking, in a fierce kind of way, with a long, lean body. I guessed he was in his early-30s, close to my age. He wasn't wearing leather, sporting instead a black, lightweight shirt of natural fibers. The collar of his shirt was open and he'd rolled up the sleeves to just below his elbows. The shirt was tucked with conscious sloppiness into a pair of dark, well-fitted jeans.

He wore his black hair in a longer style, most of it pushed behind his ears, the ends curling where they hit his shoulders. He made me think of a continental playboy. I expected him to have an accent when he spoke. Turned out, he didn't. Just a plain old American accent.

"Lilly," he said, "It's good to see you. It's been a while." He smiled when he said it. He had sexy lips, well-defined.

Lilly squirmed, nodded jerkily, then looked back down at her drink and appeared to develop a fascination with the swizzle stick, twisting it in her fingers and eyeing it uneasily.

"Who's your friend?" he asked, then turned to me.

He had the most stunning blue eyes. They were that uncommon light blue, like wolf eyes. Something uncurled in my lower belly, a twist of attraction. It wasn't at all like what I felt the first time I saw The Businessman. But it was something. It was most definitely something.

I smiled while Lilly made an awkward introduction. His name was Michael Weston. When he asked if he could sit, I readily nodded and scooted over toward the center of the booth to give him room to sit next to me.

I wanted to talk to him, but I couldn't ignore Lilly's apparent discomfort. Quickly, before Michael got settled, I whispered to her, "Is he the one who stood you up tonight?"

"No," she said, her voice clipped.

"An ex?"

"No."

"Oh," was all I said, then dropped it.

Michael leaned back in the booth beside me, his arm draping casually on the top of the back cushion. He was a man who knew how to be at ease.

"So, Nonnie, how do you know Lilly?" he asked.

I told him how we met that night, and that we decided to come check out this place because she'd been here before, and so on. He listened with keen interest and kept a friendly smile on his face.

"And what's your verdict?" he asked. "Do you think this is a sex club?"

"I have no idea. Maybe you could tell me."

"Better yet," he said, "Why don't you tell me what you hope it is?"

I smiled. I couldn't help but be flattered that this extremely attractive man was flirting with me. I thought to myself that I was on something of a roll lately.

"Well, I guess I hope it's a sex club," I answered. "If it's a regular club I won't have a good story to tell my friends when they ask what I did this weekend."

"Ah, I see. Then you're more interested in a story than the truth." His natural charm and relaxed grin took the implied sting out of his statement.

"I wouldn't say that. I was just being flippant, really."

"You're attractive when you're flippant."

Oh my. Lilly interrupted the exchange, saying she had to go to the bathroom, then rushed off.

Michael and I didn't even glance at her as she left. We chatted and lightly flirted for a few more minutes, mostly discussing the decor of the club and its patrons. Soon, the conversation turned back to the true nature of the nightclub.

He leaned toward me. "Flippancy aside, tell me, what really does interest you more? Fantasy or reality?"

"I think there's a place for both, depending on the circumstances."

He glanced down at my hands which were holding my drink, then back up at my face. "What if I were to tell you that this place both is and is not a sex club?"

"I'd say I don't know what you mean."

"It is a sex club in that some people come here to find others of a similar mindset, and to engage them sexually. For them this is real. They live a certain kind of life. Other people come here out of curiosity and find that they're unprepared for the reality of their fantasies. For them, this isn't a sex club; it's a place of titillation and fancy."

"In other words," I said, "some are tourists and some are locals."

"Exactly. And you can't tell which is which by what they're wearing."

I regarded the crowd. A woman in skintight leather pants and a vest three sizes too small tottered precariously on a pair of six-inch-high heels. Tourist or local?

"What about her?" I asked. "Which is she?"

He glanced at her then back to me. "She's a local," he said with no hesitation.

"How do you know?"

His eyes bore into mine, as if he were debating his next words. "I know because several months ago I took her into one of the rooms in the back. I stripped her naked, chained her to a rack and whipped her until I didn't feel like whipping her anymore."

Good God. I think I flinched backward. My stomach clenched. Was he serious? He was serious. No one could see his face and doubt his veracity.

I scanned the crowd to find the woman again. There she was. She seemed fine. She was flirting with an older, grey-haired man wearing khaki pants. Would he be the next man to whip her? Would he do it tonight? Would he wear those pants?

Good God.

I suddenly found it impossible to look at Michael, and I had no idea what to say.

I jumped a bit when he touched my hand, but I didn't pull away.

"It's okay that you're a tourist ... for now," he said.

I shook my head. No, I was neither tourist nor local. I was just out on a lark. "I'm ... you took me aback is all. I didn't expect —"

"Don't deny your curiosity." His tone soothed the edge off my discomfort. "How can you ever know what you want if you don't ask yourself what it might be?"

He held my hand in his large, tanned one. "Look at that lady over there, the one wearing the green sequined dress."

I saw her. I couldn't miss her, actually, what with the sparkles and all.

"She's a tourist," he said. "There are some things we might know about her. Maybe a boyfriend once gave her a playful swat on her butt while he was fucking her, and because she felt a little thrill, she wondered what it would be like if he had struck her again, harder."

"Or maybe her husband once tied her to the bedposts," he continued. "Lightly of course, so she could easily free herself if she wanted. It excited her, but she wondered what it would be like to be bound so tightly she could never free herself on her own. She wondered how it would feel to truly be at someone else's mercy, someone who could and would do as he pleased."

At some point while he spoke, I turned my eyes to his. Beautiful blue eyes. Roguish eyes making sensual promises that I had no doubt he could keep. And I thought, perhaps he was right. Maybe I was like the woman in the green dress. But he didn't know it all. He couldn't know about a dark corridor and a silken tie.

"I think you've had such moments," he said, "or something like them, and I think that's what brought you here tonight. You didn't want a story to tell your friends. You wanted an actual experience."

"Perhaps," I said, the most I was willing to admit.

"We could find out, you know."

"Nooo, not a chance. You're not strapping me down and whipping me. Hell no."

He chuckled softly and took my hand. "You misunderstand me. My mistake. I'd never treat a visitor in such a way, unless, of course, she begged me."

I gulped. "Yeah, well ..."

"No worries. You think I'm moving too fast, but that's just how we are here." He shrugged. "We've learned not to beat around the bush and waste our time on small talk, or at least not much of it. Whether you'll say it or not, you know why you're here. Everyone knows why they're here, so why pretend otherwise?"

I wondered. There was an honesty in his words that I couldn't deny. I had gone out that evening seeking a man who would probably be right at home in this club. So what did that say about me? When Lilly offered to bring me here, I didn't say no. I wanted to come and see, and not because of a silly reason like entertaining my friends.

So yes, there was truth in what he said. Yet there was also a lack of concern, a something that was too casual for me, too anonymous.

"I understand what you're saying," I said.

"Good." He squeezed my hand. "What do you say we try an experiment?"

"What kind of experiment?"

He laughed at my expression, which I'm sure was the definition of skeptical. "Only a little something to help us begin to know what it is you want."

"I don't know."

"Hear me out." One of his fingers lightly stroked my palm. I enjoyed the tiny shivers it sent up my arm.

"Okay," I said.

"I find you very attractive. I think you know this."

"I guess, yes."

"And you're attracted to me."

I reluctantly admitted that I was.

"I like many things that I can see of you," he said, "but right now, there are two things I'd like to see more of. One is here." He released my hand and ran a feathery touch across the base of my throat, near my collarbone.

I allowed it.

He continued, slow and sexy. "You're beautifully delicate right here. Many women are. It's one of my favorite spots on a woman's body. It's the hollow between your bones."

His fingers slid gently over my shoulders. "I like to imagine I've poured a spoonful of honey in that delicate place and that I'm going to lick it off of you."

Mmm. I could practically feel him doing it.

"That's one thing," he said. "The other thing is cleavage. Your breasts seem to be lovely from what I can see. They suit your frame. I'd like to see more, but not all. Not yet. I just want to see the top of your bra, to see the upper curve of your breasts and the valley between."

He leaned back into his leisurely reclined pose, picked up his drink and smiled at me. "So the experiment is this. Right here, right now, I want you to unbutton three buttons on your shirt and then pull it open far enough that I can see your collarbones and the tops of your breasts. Sounds like a fair beginning."

"But there are people everywhere. They'll see."

"So? It's not like you'll be naked."

"Well, no but —"

"Many of them are wearing practically nothing and no one's fussing about it. I assure you that showing some bra won't get you arrested for public indecency. Not here, anyway."

"What about Lilly?" I felt disconcerted and then guilty when I realized I hadn't given her a single thought since she left. Where was she? Good grief. I was as bad as my friends. "She should be coming back soon. How long has she been gone?"

"Lilly already came back," he said to my surprise. "She took a look at us, had the good manners not to interrupt and went elsewhere. Where she went, I don't know, or care."

"Really? I mean about Lilly seeing us and leaving?"

"Lilly isn't as innocent as she appears. Like you."

I had a passing thought that he and Lilly must be more than casual acquaintances, but there was a greater concern at the moment: Michael's tourist test.

"Okay, I'll forget about Lilly for now," I said. "But look, I don't know what to do ... about this test of yours."

I honestly didn't know. I wanted to do it, deep down I knew I did, but I also didn't want to. The idea made my heart beat faster. It also made me afraid. I don't think the fear was of Michael or of other people seeing me in my bra. It was a fear of something more than that.

"No problem. I'll make it simple." He slowly looked down at my breasts then back up into my eyes. "You can say no and I'll shake your hand and leave you in peace. Or, you can do as I've asked. It would please me to see more of you. It would also please me for others to see more of you."

He paused a moment to let his words sink in, then continued. "If pleasing me is appealing to you, you'll take the opportunity to do as I ask. By pleasing me, you'll please yourself, or at least, that is one thing we might discover, yes?"

I nodded.

"No rush, Think about it." He looked away from me and sipped his drink, nonchalant as his gaze wandered over the club at large.

I reached for the top button of my blouse and stopped there. It was only three buttons. Just three. What would it be like to do this? It was nothing. Practically nothing anyway. I wanted to know what it would feel like, to do this little thing he asked. To please him. To please myself.

I unbuttoned the top button. No harm in it. It showed nothing. Then the second button. I revealed some cleavage. Nothing much. But the third button ...

I couldn't bear to check out who might be watching me. I wasn't even positive that Michael watched me, I was so focused on that third button. Heat rose up my neck as I considered what I would do. That button seemed a long way down my shirt. Well below my breastbone. If I undid it I'd expose more than just the top of my bra.

I took a breath, and I unbuttoned the third button.

Michael's voice jarred me. "Excellent. Now spread your blouse open so I can see what I wanted to see."

I looked over at him, but he was watching my hands. Slowly, I opened my shirt, revealing my chest to him. I laid the shirt back and down, creating a long deep V that showed pretty much everything. My bra was a demi-cup, so if it was cleavage he wanted, he certainly got it.

A lazy smile played across Michael's face as he perused my shoulders and breasts. "Beautiful. And a relief. I'm glad to see it's all you filling those cups."

My face grew hotter. "God, that's embarrassing. You wanted to see if I stuff my bra? We're not in high school."

"I don't care if it's embarrassing. I wanted to know."

I felt a lurch between my legs. "How long do I have to stay like this?"

"You can stop whenever you want, but if you want to make me happy, you'll leave your shirt open, drop your hands to your lap and leave them there until I tell you otherwise."

It was the casual way he said it. Casual, yes, but with an unmistakable undertone of command. It reminded me of my time in a dark corridor with a different, forceful man. The trembling sensation in my stomach increased.

I did as Michael asked.

He said nothing. He only looked, a leisurely exploration of my shoulders and the rounded tops of my breasts. It thrilled and embarrassed me at the same time. He was pleased. I saw that. And he was right, in that his pleasure was clearly doing something for me as well. I felt strung tight and his attention plucked the strings.

The rest of the room faded away, and it was only me and Michael, until he said, "I want you to look into the crowd and see who's looking back."

Of course, I thought. The crowd. The people who might be watching. He wanted them to see me as much as he himself wanted to see. I moved my eyes toward the rest of the room, but I didn't actually attend to the details. Basically, I cheated.

He wasn't fooled. "Look at them. I can tell you aren't."

I itched to diffuse the sexual tension between us by challenging him, lying and telling him he was wrong. Cowardice on my part. I took a breath to ready myself, and then I looked, actually saw what was there to see.

"Many people are looking at you," Michael said, his warm voice like a stimulant. "The people who know this is a sex club are thinking I'm a lucky man to have found someone with potential."

Though there were at least several hundred people in the club, no more than thirty or forty of them were in a position to see me, and not all of them were looking in my direction. Still, it seemed an enormous number of potential voyeurs.

I saw them, then, the men and women regarding my breasts. But they weren't just looking there, at the obvious. They watched my face, looked into my eyes as well. As I met one person's gaze then moved to the next, I saw they understood what I was just beginning to grasp.

A feeling pulsed inside me. It shortened my breath and my blood thrummed through my veins, a luscious wave of sensation that I would never stop of my own will.

I knew the thrumming in my body wasn't caused by embarrassment that strangers were staring at my cleavage. I knew it. And I knew that Michael and the others weren't solely turned on by the display of some flesh.

It was sensual and thrilling not just because of the result, but mostly because of the action, the doing of it. I had done as he asked, and I did it because it pleased him. Even though I was embarrassed. Even though a big part of me didn't want to, I did it anyway.

I put myself on display because he wished it. And the unasked question floating between me and my audience was, what else would I do to please him?

I think Michael must have sensed my revelation. He reached out and ran a finger along the edge of my bra, tantalizing the tops of my breasts. I didn't stop him. I wanted him to do as he pleased, now, to keep the heat rushing through me.

He hooked a lone finger under the filmy lace at the top of my bra. Pushing farther down under the fabric, the back of his fingernail rubbed against my nipple. I didn't need to look down to see what he was doing. I watched the crowd, like he wanted me to do.

He made a sound of enjoyment as the back of his finger stroked me and my nipple went hard, an animate tingling thing. The people watching no longer regarded my face. Their interest lay in what Michael was doing to my breast, under the cover of white lace.

Some of them smiled lazily, some leered, some wanted to be me, and some of them wanted to be Michael, or to join him. The thought didn't frighten me. It excited me. I was with Michael alone. The other people only got what he gave them.

Michael's touches raised the game to a different level. I was in the thrall of this new thing, this new experience. My senses were on full alert. I felt the driving beat of the dance music. I smelled Michael's cologne and the sweetness of the remains of my cocktail, the sharp scent of my aroused and heated skin. I felt every millimeter of Michael's finger, the smooth arc of its rise and fall over my breast, the curious pressure of his touch, the tweak of a fingernail's scratch as it passed the sides of my nipple.

I was living a fantasy I never knew I had. My body was keyed to the moment. What would Michael do next? Would I allow it? How far would I go for his pleasure? How far would I go for my own?

And then I saw Him. I was drinking the attention of the crowd when I saw him. He stood next to a grouping of nearby tables, and he was watching me. His dark hair was brushed back from his forehead. His jaw was taut, and his body seemed coiled with strength.

He met my eyes with an expression of anger that made me wince involuntarily. Anger. At who? At me?

It was The Businessman.

« CHAPTER 4 »

IN THE EIGHTH YEAR OF my marriage, I had an affair with a
man who lived in the apartment above mine. His name was Doug, and
he was a senior in college. Because I married at a young age, only eighteen years old, Doug wasn't much younger than I.

He was lovely and what I thought I needed at the time. He
adored me. Or rather, he adored my body. When he looked at me naked, his features slackened, as if the lines and curves of my figure short-
circuited his brain cells.

I was flattered. He made me feel beautiful and wanted. So I slept
with him every chance I got for nearly two months. When I told him it
was over, he cried. Sweet young man. He thought he loved me.

When my ex-husband and I were first married, we had sex all
the time, common for newlyweds. The sex was okay for me, and I
thought it would get better in time. It didn't. I never told my ex that
being intimate with him wasn't as enthralling as I wished; his glass-thin
ego never could stand the weakest knock of complaint. So I faked it. If
he wanted sex, he got it. Luckily for me, as time went on, he wanted it
less and less.

The week before I began my affair with Doug, my ex had
climbed into our bed late one night while I was sleeping, and with hardly a grunt of acknowledgement, proceeded to have sex with me. He
rolled me onto my back, pushed up my nightgown, shoved the crotch
of my panties to one side, spat in his palm, rubbed the spit on his penis, then climbed between my legs and shoved himself inside me.

His closed his eyes while he fucked me. It was over in a few
minutes. He came, rolled off of me, then stood up and left the room.
He never said a word to me, nor I to him.

I lay in the bed, immobile, legs sprawled open, his semen slowly seeping out of me onto my bunched-up panties. When the goo cooled and became clammy, I got up and took a shower.

I didn't think about anything while I cleaned myself and changed the sheets. What was there to think about? I knew why he did it. It was because I dared to suggest, again, that he might look for a job. My bad. Guess I had it coming. I was a bitch. A fellow deserved a little something to make him feel better after his wife insulted his manhood, didn't he?

I didn't actually believe any of that bullshit. That was his side of things, and I knew it well. Over the next week, I asked myself, "If you know you didn't do anything wrong, then why did you let him do that to you?"

I was standing in the stairwell of our apartment building, heading home from work, when the answer finally came to me — it was easier to bear my husband's vile behavior than it was to try to change it, effort which would only result in pointless argument.

Could it be that simple? Yes. I didn't care about him anymore. I felt nothing, not when he talked to me and certainly not when he touched me. The night he "chastised" me, the only thing I felt was that damned, cold semen.

I stood in the stairwell thinking it through, wondering how many years I'd been numb, when Doug came jogging down the stairs. He ran the way young men do, young men with more energy than sense. He smiled at me and said hello in the flirtatious way he always spoke to me. I never encouraged him ... not until that day.

I thought, Doug can make me feel something. So I encouraged him, and instead of going home to my husband, I went upstairs with Doug.

He was my indulgence. Even more delightful than his adoration was the knowledge that our time together belonged to me, that my husband couldn't take it from me.

I liked Doug to fuck me in positions where I could see a door, any door. Doggy style was a favorite. Me, on the floor on my hands and knees, with Doug pumping away at me from behind, his hands roaming over my ass and back.

His apartment smelled of unwashed clothes, dirty dishes and half-eaten delivery pizzas. But I didn't care. I didn't care that the furniture was a collection of stained cast-offs and that Doug undoubtedly never vacuumed the shabby carpet that rubbed faint burns on my knees and reddened my palms.

None of it mattered because Doug, himself, smelled of soap and herbal shampoo, layered with the delicious scent of honest desire. On my hands and knees, I would crane my neck to see him behind me, all clean and new, his skin shining with health and a thin sheen of sweat, a testament to passionate vigor.

But mostly, I kept my sight trained on the door in front of me. I imagined my husband kicking the door open and barging inside, seeing me and my lover in our adulterous glory. I pictured my wastrel of a mate gawping at me in surprise. He never suspected something like this from me. Never.

And I would shoo him away, saying, "Go home. There's nothing for you here."

And he'd know it was true, so he'd turn around and slump out the door, still surprised and confused but understanding there was nothing to be gained from outrage, or even further discussion.

Sometimes I varied the scenes, played out different scenarios, but the gist of my reaction to his discovery was always the same. An offhand "Fuck you."

I never felt guilty about my affair with Doug. I never would.

Now, here I was, years later, sitting in a sex club. A man who looked liked a continental playboy had a finger in my bra and was toying with my nipple while a couple dozen club-goers enjoyed the show.

Then I saw The Businessman among the watching crowd, looking as devastatingly handsome as I remembered. And he was angry. Definitely angry.

Immediately, I felt guilty.

Guilt. Really? It couldn't be. The memory of cheating on my husband blazed clear and large in my mind. I'd felt no guilt for a cuckolded husband, for broken vows and secret trysts. Not even once. Not even close.

Apparently, I saved my shame for virtual strangers, for men who seduced me then didn't bother to tell me their names, or ask for mine.

What the hell was wrong with me? The entire scene was absurd to the point of farce. I fought down an urge to laugh, though I was in no way amused.

I couldn't look away from The Businessman and his anger. Mixed with my inexplicable feelings of guilt was an equally inexplicable, though less powerful, tremble of fear. Fear of what? Shame for what?

He and I didn't even know each other, not in any real way. There could be no concerns about promises and fidelity. Yet he glared at me as if I'd somehow betrayed him. Impossible.

Michael noticed the change in me. He followed my gaze to The Businessman, who immediately switched his glare from me to Michael.

Michael smiled and gave an acknowledgement nod, the briefest hello. The Businessman didn't return the gesture. His angry expression disappeared the next instant, replaced by total blandness. He turned away and walked off into the crowd, gone from my view within seconds.

Now you see him, now you don't, I thought. How like him.

Michael, still smiling, appeared unfazed by The Businessman's cut. His finger circled my nipple as he asked, "Someone you know?"

The moment having been considerably dampened for me, I gently removed his hand from my breast and answered, "A passing acquaintance."

Mood spoiled, I buttoned up my shirt.

Michael sighed in a playfully dramatic way. "It's so sad when a good time is ruined by some random thing or other. Still, you pleased me while it lasted, so I'm content with that."

I smiled even though my nerves remained on edge. I reached for my drink. It was watery and tasteless from the melted ice, but it served its purpose of wetting my dry lips and mouth, bringing me back to a more even state.

I asked the question that I wasn't sure I wanted answered. "Do you know that man?"

I was certain that Michael almost asked, "Who?" It was something about the shape of his mouth before he said, "Just a passing acquaintance, same as you."

"Do you know his name? I can't remember it, and I hate it when I can't remember a name."

Michael said he didn't remember. I was disappointed, until Michael added, "But I've heard some rumors about him."

Ah, rumors. That was something, anyway. "Oh," I said, then waited to see if he would tell me more.

He did. "Some people have said he can be, how should I say this, unfeeling and harsh to his, uh, to the women under his care."

"What do you mean, the women under his care?"

"His sexual partners. I'm not much for labels, but in general, a partner of his would be called a sub, short for submissive."

This time my "Oh" was no ploy. "Then he's some kind of regular here, and has subs. It's BDSM."

"Most people who come here are into BDSM," he said, "in one way or another, as I more or less told you before. I'm pleased you know the term. You'd be surprised how many people don't. Here I thought you were an innocent young thing with no idea of the ways of the world."

"Uh-huh. Was that before or after you stuck your finger in my bra in front of 30-odd strangers?"

He chuckled low and sexy, "Well, perhaps not all that innocent. Innocent enough that I thought you needed special handling. Now, however ..."

I didn't like where he was heading. "I don't live under a rock, so I have a general knowledge of what BDSM is. Whips, chains, whatever. But I don't know anything other than what I've seen in movies or tv."

Michael grew thoughtful and studied me. "You're right. There are whips and chains in BDSM, but they're just tools. A means to an end."

A means to an end. I wasn't sure that bore much thinking about, not at the moment anyway.

I said what I'd not yet had the chance to say. "That man we were talking about. The one with the rumors. You said he was unfeeling and harsh to his partners. Does that mean he dumps a lot of women, or does it mean he ... physically harms ..." I didn't know how to finish my sentence.

"No idea," Michael said. "It could mean many things, or nothing. It's only rumors. I find it interesting, though, that the conversation keeps coming back to him. How did you meet him?"

From his clipped tone, I knew this was a question he dearly wanted answered. "I don't remember," I said.

"Hmm. Interesting." His arm had been draped casually over the back of the booth. It wasn't a stretch for him to reach out and touch my hair, twirling one of my curls around his finger. "You shouldn't wonder that I'm curious about you and him. Perhaps it was my imagination, but I think he was angry when he saw us together. At first, I thought that he snubbed me because he was in a foul mood or some other nonsense. But now I wonder. Was he angry because you were here with someone other than him?"

"I don't see how that could be possible. We don't even really know each other."

Michael misread my rising agitation. He gave my hair a teasing tug and smiled. "Don't be annoyed with me. You can't blame me for feeling a little jealous, can you? It's nothing serious. It's only that tonight, by the best of luck, I found the loveliest woman I've met in a long time. All I want to do is talk with her some more about pleasure, while all she wants to do is talk about another man."

My first reaction was to assure him that I wasn't offended and that I hadn't been thinking about The Businessman. But I stopped before I said anything. I would never admit it to him, but Michael was right about me digging for information. Why was I doing that, anyway?

The Businessman's anger, like my guilt, was irrational. According to rumors, he treated women badly. I wasn't going to be able to ask Michael for specifics about those rumors. Regardless, the critical point was that The Businessman walked away from me yet again.

Michael was here. I was undeniably attracted to him. Who wouldn't be? I loved the way his long hair brushed his shoulders and the way he pushed it behind his ears with casual unconcern. His body was lean, taut and strong. And maybe he was a bit dangerous, too. Who knew where he could lead me. He was persuasive, to say the least.

I went out that night to pursue a desire that The Businessman had created. There was no reason why he had to be the one to fulfill it. Michael Weston could do just as well. Maybe better. I wouldn't know without trying.

"I'm sorry I've given you the wrong impression. I'm not interested in that man," I said.

"I'm glad to hear it."

"I'm just worried that I might have wandered into something that's out of my depth. The idea of BDSM is, well, let's just say, I'm not a masochist, and I'm certainly not a sadist."

"How do you know?"

I laughed at this ridiculous question. "I think I'd know if I were. If I knock my shin on a coffee table, it just hurts, it doesn't turn me on. And I've definitely never been excited by someone else's pain. I can't even imagine it."

I recalled how it felt when The Businessman spanked me and I almost withdrew my statement. Those smacks felt nothing like a banged-up shin.

"You laugh," he said, "but it's only because you don't understand. I could talk to you for hours about how you're wrong, but it would be much easier to show you."

I thought of the woman in the stiletto heels, the woman Michael said he'd whipped. I shook my head. "I'm not looking for a beating tonight."

Michael gave a rueful chuckle. "That's a pity. But I didn't think you were. I believe we've proven you like to be watched, though, and I believe the next logical step is to see if you like to watch others, too. It could serve the additional purpose of a lesson, if you're interested in learning more."

One of the things that most intrigued me about Michael was his ability to make outrageous offers seem perfectly logical. Normal even. He said all of the above as if he were suggesting we take in a tennis match because I mentioned I'd never seen the game.

I didn't know what to say to him.

Fortunately, I didn't have to come up with anything.

"It would be a simple thing," he said. "Right before I came over here I saw some old friends heading to the back. We could go watch them. Trust me when I tell you, they wouldn't mind. It's why they're here, after all."

I couldn't deny that I was tempted. Hell, Michael was a seductive enticement in his own right.

"How would it work?" I asked. "Is it like an arena or something? Or do we just knock on the door and say, hey there, we want to watch you do whatever it is you're doing?"

He smiled. "No. We'd be in a different room. Just you and me. Alone."

He waved his hand in the air, as if to brush aside any further questions or objections I might have. "It's no big deal. You'll see. We'll just go back there and you can take a look around. If you don't want to stay, you're always free to walk away. Consider it a complimentary tour of the club."

"Well ..."

Then he sealed the deal. "You enjoyed pleasing me before. Say yes, and you'll please me again."

I weakened. "Maybe, but first, I need a drink." I said it in a teasing way, but I was serious too. Had I ever needed a drink more? I didn't think so.

Michael's flirtatious demeanor changed. His brows lowered. "How many drinks have you already had tonight?"

"Three, maybe four. I don't see how it's any concern of —"

"Then you've had more than plenty. And it is my concern. You want another drink so that when you wake up with a hangover tomorrow morning you can blame whatever happens tonight on the alcohol. If you do that, you'll cheat yourself out of what you learn here, and make it a waste of time. Are you wanting to waste my time?"

"No, of course not. I was just ..." I almost said "kidding around," but that wasn't true. I thought I was kidding around, but maybe he was right. I didn't know. Once again, he was a persuasive man, and he elicited an inexplicable urge in me to give him what he wanted.

"Do you still want that drink?" he asked.

"I guess not."

I felt a small flutter when, at my answer, he smiled. "Good, let's go."

I thought, I guess I'm doing this thing. I could always leave. That's what he promised. I'd hold him to it.

We slid out of the booth, and he pressed his hand against the small of my back, guiding me through the crowd to the rear of the room, then through the open doorframe marked VIP. Not far inside, the short hallway ended in a closed door which was attended by a man who might have been a twin of the beefy bouncer guarding the club's entrance.

Michael nodded at the man. The guard returned his nod, opened the door then stepped aside to allow us to enter.

My nerves a-jangle, I allowed Michael to lead me into the unknown.

« Chapter 5 »

We entered a hallway which was surprisingly well-lit. I guess I'd been expecting cheesy red lights, paintings of nude women and worn runner carpets, your basic movie-whorehouse decor. There weren't even any tables crowded with celebrity wannabes swilling down over-priced champagne.

Instead I was met with a wide hallway that could be found in any modern business complex. The walls were covered with beige textured wallpaper that would be at home in a nice office. The carpeting was deep blue and of the sturdy variety you see in public places. A pleasant citrus aroma filled the air.

I could have been walking down this hallway to visit an accountant, or a doctor.

We made a left turn and came upon a young woman seated at a desk. She was a sweet-looking girl, with bouncy brown curls, and freckles scattered across her nose. She wore a demure cotton dress and was painting her nails a garish purple, though she stopped immediately when she saw us turn the corner.

She glanced up at us, then immediately back down to the desk, where she quickly put the top back on the bottle of polish.

She stood as if she were at military attention. "Sir," was the only word she said when we stopped in front of her. She kept her eyes on the desk and didn't look up at us again.

"Are the Hoytes in a session?" Michael asked.

"Yes, Sir. They're in room seven."

"I'd like a viewing room, then, if one's open."

"Yes, Sir."

She reached into a desk drawer and came up with a card that reminded me of the kind you get at hotels, an electronic door key. "Room 7E, Sir."

Michael took the key and thanked her. The girl's posture relaxed. She stiffened again when he said, "By the way, Sarah, I didn't ask what room the Hoytes were in. I'm not a big stickler on these things, but there are others who wouldn't appreciate your presumption."

She looked aghast. "I'm sorry, Sir. I should have been more careful. I know I shouldn't presume."

Michael blew out a bored-sounding sigh. "I said it's not about me. Go back to your nails."

"Yes, Sir. Thank you, Sir." And she dropped back into her chair and grabbed the bottle of polish as if her life depended on it.

We walked off. When we were far enough away that I figured Sarah wouldn't be able to hear, I whispered, "What was that about?"

"It was nothing. The owners like using trainees to man the desk and we're supposed to do our parts in their training. It's a bother."

"Training?"

"It's a formal thing that some Doms do. It's not important right now."

We took several more turns down lengthy hallways until we came to a door marked with the number seven, and then past number seven to a door with a sign that read, "Viewing Rooms," and underneath that, "7A - 7E and 8A - 8E."

Michael opened the door and we entered into another hallway, this one narrower and lined with doors, seven's on one side, eight's on the other. We went to the one labeled 7E, where Michael used his card key and ushered me inside.

It was a small room, only large enough to hold an oversized recliner, a cushioned bench, a small end table, and of all things, a chaise longue. The furniture was covered in a sturdy, black vinyl. I thought it was a good choice, that it would be easy to keep clean. This was not a strange thought to have, considering one of the odors in the room.

Mostly, the room smelled of an exotic Asian blend of incense. But under that smell was the barely perceptible tang of disinfectant, an obvious declaration of the room's purpose. I should have been comforted and reassured by this sign of cleanliness. Instead, I became a tangle of nerves and anticipation, a condition that worsened the longer I examined the room.

It was as brightly lit as a kitchen, the walls and floor shining pristine white under the glare. The huge curtain was white, too, stretching from sidewall to sidewall and ceiling to floor on the far side. I assumed the curtain covered the window into Room 7.

In all, it reminded me of a surgical viewing room, not comforting in the slightest.

Michael gave me a reassuring smile. He took my purse and laid it on the little table, then turned a knob on the wall, a dimmer for the lights as it turned out. As shadows took shape around the furniture, the softer light soothed the harsh sterility of the room.

"Better?" he asked.

I nodded.

"I know, the decorating scheme is austere. In its defense, it's intended to let you know how clean it is, so there's no doubt."

"Mission accomplished," I said.

He opened a door in the base of the side table. It was a mini fridge. "Are you thirsty? Water, juice, soda?"

I shook my head no.

He closed the door and walked over to me. The demeanor of polite cordiality dropped away as he reached out and ran his fingers down the length of my bare arm.

His voice was low and warm. "It's okay if you're nervous, and a bit scared. It excites me."

He put his arms around my waist and gently pulled me closer. "Remember, you can always walk away. The door is only locked to the outside. You're free to leave any time you wish."

"I'll remember," I said, my voice sounding strange in my head, reedy and thin.

He was tall, my head reaching just shy of his chin. He leaned down and whispered near my ear, "You don't have to do anything. I know what needs to be done. Trust me and let me guide you. You'll be fine."

He soothed me with more honeyed words, and pressed soft kisses on my ear lobe. He told me to relax, to enjoy the moment. I put my arms around his neck and did as he said. It was easy, with him.

Apparently, we were here to do more than watch, but I was no fool. I'd figured as much. And Michael was handsome, thrilling in a new way. It was no difficult task to enjoy what he did to me.

His warm breath played across my neck and his hands caressed my back. Then he kissed me, his lips light and gentle on my own. His scent was a masculine musk.

Then his tongue reached out to test me. We tasted one another. He tasted of fresh oranges, rum and a hint of mint.

He unbuttoned my shirt, kissing me all the while. I let it happen, wanted it to happen, so when he slipped it from my shoulders, and headed straight for the clasp of my bra, I didn't try to slow him down. Slow was the last thing I wanted.

He unclasped the bra and whisked it away, then cupped my breasts, lifting them, feeling the weight. When he had touched me earlier in the evening, I hoped there might be more. Here was the more. I sighed and pressed against him.

He tasted my breasts with lips and tongue and made a sound that might have been "yes," but I couldn't be sure. My breath grew ragged and loud.

I wanted his skin next to mine, so I reached out and tugged at his shirt. He stopped nuzzling me long enough to let me remove his shirt, then he returned his attention to my breasts. I ran my hands over his smooth chest, my palms playing over the defined muscles of his lean torso.

While he sucked my hard nipples into his mouth, his hands moved to my waist, and in a moment, he unzipped my skirt and let it pool around my feet.

I reached for his belt then, wanting to see more of him, but I had no more than touched the buckle when Michael grabbed my wrists. "No."

He pushed my arms behind my back and restrained them with one of his large hands clamped around my wrists. With his other hand, he grabbed the hair at the nape of my neck and pulled my head back until I was looking up into his cold blue eyes. I felt a shiver of delicious fear rush over me.

"Time to lay down some ground rules," he said. "This isn't what you're used to, I know, but I bet you're a quick learner. Are you?"

I said I was. I damned well hoped I was.

"I allowed you to take off my shirt," he said. "That was the only boon you'll get from me tonight. Anything else that happens, and I do mean anything, will be at my direction, my command. You'll do nothing without my permission. Do you understand?"

His gaze bore into mine. I wanted this. Strange and unfamiliar as it was, I wanted it, like I'd wanted The Businessman to have his way with me in the hall. I wanted to give myself over to something bigger and stronger than myself. To let him take charge.

"Yes, I understand," I said.

He claimed my mouth, his tongue thrusting past my lips.

He released my hair and grasped one of my breasts, squeezing tighter than before. He kneaded my flesh between his fingers. Mmm. It was good to be taken by him.

Then he stopped kissing and massaging. He released my wrists.

He stepped back from me. "Put your hands behind your head. Yes, like that. Kick away the skirt. Now spread your legs. A little wider. Yes, like that. Put more arch in your back. I want your ass and tits out. Do it!"

I complied with his orders as quickly as I could. He moved various parts of me around until he had me in the pose he wanted.

He slowly circled me then, eyeing me up and down. It was embarrassing, but sensual too, standing here in front of him, wearing only panties.

"Look at the floor, or the ceiling," he said. "I don't care which. Just don't look at me unless I tell you to."

I did as he asked, staring at the floor, and though I wasn't allowed to watch him directly, I could see what he was doing well enough with my peripheral vision.

He stood beside me. "This is position number one." He reached out and rubbed my ass cheek. With his other hand he cupped one of my breasts then ran his fingers down my abdomen, pausing above the flimsy triangle of white silk between my legs.

"Remember this pose," he said.

"Yes." I wanted his hand to slip lower, under the silk.

"Don't move," he said.

Then he moved. I kept my eyes on the floor until I heard a loud sound behind me, a scraping sound. Without moving my torso, I turned my head a fraction of an inch to see what he was doing. He was pushing the cushioned bench into the center of the room. I returned my gaze to the floor in front of me.

When he finished, he slipped an arm around my waist from behind and pulled me against him. His other hand roamed freely over my breasts. I arched my back, a subconscious push of my breasts into his hand. We both breathed harder. I thought this was because of what he was doing to me, but I was wrong, about him, anyway.

His whisper was filled with menace. "I told you not to move, and you've already disobeyed me twice."

I shivered. "I didn't mean to, I —"

"Don't make it worse with excuses, Sweet. I don't tolerate disobedience. If you weren't a beginner, this might have gone very, very badly for you. But as it is, your punishment will be light."

I thought, my punishment? Oh, hell.

"Now listen closely, because I won't repeat this warning," he continued, still using that menacing whisper. "Do not disobey me a third time. If you do, the repercussions will be ... severe. Do you understand?"

I nodded, my head feeling big and wobbly on my neck.

"Words," he said.

"Yes," I managed to say, somehow.

"Good." He abruptly released me. "Now go straddle that bench."

I moved as if I were in someone else's body, someone else's dream. It seemed as if the more demanding Michael became, the more I wanted to obey. My reaction to him flew in the face of what I thought I knew about my character, defied who I thought I was. I felt much the same way as I did when I was with The Businessman. I'd think, why am I doing this? And then I'd go do it without pausing for an answer.

Michael instructed me in how he wanted me to straddle the backless bench. It sat in the center of the room, lengthwise, with one end facing the curtained wall. I was forced to spread my legs wide to straddle the bench and didn't feel wholly secure on my feet when Michael nudged me to move up more.

Attached to the end of the bench was a raised bar which I had originally thought was an arm rest. Perhaps it was an arm rest, but that wasn't the purpose Michael had for it. He instructed me to bend over and grab the bar with both hands. He adjusted the position of my feet and the arch of my back and neck, the straightness of my legs, until he had me where he wanted me.

It was a position of intimate exposure. I wasn't tied or restrained in any way, but he made me feel as if I were. The muscles in my calves and thighs stretched taut from the angle of my heels conflicting with my bent torso and arched back, from the extreme spread demanded by the width of the bench. My ass jutted out, my pussy and anus covered only by the thinnest of silk.

Michael made a grunt which I assumed meant he was satisfied, then stood in front of me. "Don't remove your hands from that bar unless I tell you to. Do you understand?"

I told him I did then watched, fascinated when he began to unbuckle his belt, his crotch mere inches from my face. I felt a rush of wetness between my legs.

He pulled his belt from the loops of his jeans. He didn't drop the belt as I thought he would, nor did he begin to unfasten his jeans. Instead, he doubled the belt between his hands.

After walking around behind me, he massaged one of my ass cheeks.

"Before we can watch the show in the main room, there's something you have to understand," he said.

He squeezed and rubbed each of my buttocks in turn, like he was testing my flesh, testing the spring of skin and muscle over bone. "You're going to see a woman getting whipped. Have you ever been whipped, Sweet?"

I managed to say no, not easy since I'd been holding my breath.

"To have any chance of understanding what the woman in the other room is feeling," he said, "you need to have some experience. Not a great deal, but some point of reference. I'm not going to whip you, of course. It's too soon for that. A few light rounds with my belt, however, might be of some use to you."

And with that, he snapped the belt across my ass. I bit back a squeal, but made a grunting noise all the same. Fire flashed across my ass, gone again in a moment.

Michael rubbed where he hit me. Then smack! The belt struck again. Smack! Again. I grunted with the blows.

He rubbed me, "Her ass will be bare, of course. And she'll feel so much more pain than this, you can't imagine."

He struck again. I clenched my stomach against the growing burn. My ass became more sensitive with each strike, or perhaps the strikes themselves were becoming harder. Then he rubbed me again. His hand slipped under my panties, skin on skin, and he slid his fingers down the crack of my ass, then lower to my pussy, my embarrassingly wet pussy.

He stroked me and I squirmed under his touch. I forgot about the belt and the burn.

I shouldn't have. In a quick motion, his hand was gone and once again the belt struck, but this time lower, where the bottom of my buttocks met the tops of my thighs. I barely contained my cry.

Michael chuckled. "That one was for turning your head when I told you not to."

He struck again, the same spot, with greater force than he'd used yet. I was unable, finally, to restrain a yelp. My skin stung and burned from the blow.

"That was for arching your back when I told you to hold your position. Just think, you never would have gotten those two blows if you hadn't been disobedient."

"Of course," he said, "I get my greatest pleasure when you obey me. But, I also get pleasure when you don't. I enjoy the cries of beautiful women, Nonnie. For me, it's a win-win. Now, sit down. And remember, don't take your hands from the bar until I tell you to."

I sat down with relief and trepidation. My legs had grown increasingly trembly from the stress of holding my straight-legged position under the shock of Michael's blows, so I welcomed the respite. But my butt was fiery from the belt, and it wasn't exactly pleasant to sit at that moment. Sit I did, however, and made certain my hands stayed clasped around the bar as I changed position.

Michael straddled the bench behind me, and snugged up against my back. The warmth of his smooth chest was soothing, unlike the stinging heat plaguing my butt.

"Time for the show," he said, and pushed a button on a remote control he held.

I didn't know if I was ready, but no matter, the curtain was opening.

The window was huge, encompassing almost the entirety of the wall. The window provided an unimpeded view of the space beyond. And quite a view it was.

The room was large, with white ceiling, floor and walls, the whiteness only broken by shelves, rolling carts and various equipment of unknown purpose that neatly lined two of the walls.

Some tall lamps were scattered here and there, but weren't being used at the moment. All the lighting came from recessed fixtures in the ceiling. Plenty of hooks of various sizes and shapes adorned the ceiling as well. From one particularly strong and thick hook hung what I thought was a block and tackle. I didn't think it prudent to ponder its use. Indeed, most of the equipment in the room left me wondering at its purpose, but as with the block and tackle, I didn't spend time contemplating it.

The real display, anyway, was in the center of the room.

There were three people, two women and a man.

The man was massive in every way, thick and burly, like a professional wrestler from long ago, or a muscled dockhand. His barrel chest and meaty arms were bare. Dark hair covered his arms and torso and led down to a good-sized stomach which protruded more than a little, yet appeared tight and hard. No one would ever dare to suggest the man was fat.

His black leather pants fit him nicely and not too tightly. He wore studded black leather boots.

As if all of this weren't intimidating enough, he wore a black leather hood that fit around the entirety of his head and neck, so there was no way to know what he looked like. The only holes in the mask were for his eyes, ears, nostrils and mouth. Nothing suggested expression of any kind, leaving him devoid of the usual signs of humanity.

He resembled an executioner from another age. Instead of an axe, he held a thin black rod. He was frightening, indeed.

A woman kneeled on the floor not far away from him. She was miniscule in comparison to the bulk of the masked man. Her head was bowed and her medium-length brown hair fell forward to shield much of her face. I guessed her age at around 40. She had a ripe figure that swelled out of her tightly-cinched corset and hip-hugging skirt. The outfit was made of black leather, like the man's. Her feet were bare.

And then there was the centerpiece of the room — she was stretched on a wooden rack that stood upright, secured to the floor with support beams at the rear of the structure. The woman stretched spread-eagled on the rack, face forward, completely naked. Thick leather bracelets circled her wrists and ankles and were clipped to the four corners of the rack.

Her face was plain, free of cosmetics of any kind. Although she wasn't particularly pretty, she wasn't without attraction. Her blonde hair was secured in a low ponytail at the base of her neck. Her best feature was her eyes, large doe eyes that seemed made to portray suffering.

What she might have lacked by way of true facial beauty, she more than made up for with her slender figure. Her arms were thin and fine. She had a graceful, long neck. Her breasts were much larger than mine, and the shape of them told me they were natural. She had a small, nipped-in waist and gently rounded hips that curved down to some of the longest legs I'd ever seen. Her crotch was shaved bare.

Her skin shone in the light, glistening in a way that made me certain she was covered in some kind of oil. Several narrow red lines crisscrossed her stomach and thighs.

When the hooded man stood next to her, she seemed tiny and utterly defenseless. She was spread wide open, completely vulnerable, so vulnerable that I felt a moment's fear for her.

"Close your eyes," Michael said.

That was about the last thing I wanted to do at the moment, but I did as he asked. He wrapped something silky around my head and over my eyes. He secured it snugly from behind. I was blindfolded.

And I waited for an explanation.

Michael obliged. "The man you saw is my friend, Ron Hoyte, and the woman on her knees is his wife, Elaine. I don't know who the lovely lady on the rack is. I wasn't expecting a third person. Hoyte must have found a new toy I haven't heard about yet."

He sounded amused by the new "toy." "The red lines you saw on her body are from Hoyte's rod. We can assume, with what I know about Hoyte, that he already whipped her back and ass. He always beats back to front."

Michael chuckled then, as if this were funny. I couldn't imagine. I tried not to imagine, in fact, what the woman's back looked like.

"I hope you got a look at that rod Hoyte was holding," he said.

I said I had.

"Hoyte designed it himself. It's made of a springy graphite composite. It's thin and flat and strikes a painful sting. It leaves bright red stripes and a lasting burn. The marks fade quickly, less than a day usually. I tried it out on my leg, and it stung like hell."

"I think it's time for some audio," he said, and I assumed he used the remote control again because the sound of a woman whimpering flooded into the room.

The speakers must have been hidden somewhere in the ceiling, I thought, nonsensically.

Michael's arms wrapped around my waist, and he explored my body, his hands sliding from my stomach to the undercurves of my breasts. "Hoyte's new toy is whimpering. Can you tell if it's from pain, or pleasure?"

I listened, but I didn't know.

His fingers brushed my thighs, a light, tickling touch. "Since Hoyte was stroking her thighs, I have to believe it's pleasure."

Then a loud cracking sound split the air. Crack! I jumped. The woman cried out. Now that, I thought, was pain. Another smack, then rapidly two more. Crack! Crack! I flinched with every blow, the remaining heat on my ass a reminder of Michael's recent belting.

My breathing and heartbeat grew faster, caused not just by what I heard, but also by what I felt. Michael hands roamed my body, no, rather, kneaded my body. My inner thighs, stomach and hips, then up to my breasts. The blindfold seemed to increase the thrill of his touch, and goosebumps formed on my arms.

The woman's cries changed to the whimpering sound, then moans.

I heard a man, presumably Hoyte, say, "Slave, more oil!"

Michael explained. "That's what he calls his wife, Elaine, when they're in scenes."

I only vaguely took in this information, since I was lost amid the incongruity of Michael's touch and the whipped woman's pain.

He described the scene. "Elaine is rubbing oil on the other woman's body, her belly and legs and breasts. She has lovely big breasts. Yours are more my type, but still, hers are lovely."

He squeezed my breasts and gently pinched my nipples while he said this. I think I moaned.

"Elaine has finished oiling up Hoyte's toy," he continued. "She's back in her spot, kneeling on the floor. Hoyte is tickling his toy with the end of his rod, tickling her pussy."

I held my breath when Michael reached between my spread legs and began stroking me over my panties. His fingers teased around the elastic edge of the fabric.

Then ... crack! Hoyte struck again. I flinched. At the same time, Michael gave me a nasty little pinch on my inner thigh.

I believe I yelped louder than the woman being whipped, from surprise more than from the minor bite of his pinch.

Michael left me no time to think about it. He fondled my labia and I squirmed against him.

"I think you're beginning to see," he said, and he removed my blindfold.

I blinked. There they were, still just past the glass wall, Ron Hoyte and his two women.

"Watch them," Michael said. "Don't look away."

While Michael teased my breasts and pussy, I watched Hoyte tease the woman stretched on the rack. With the tip of the black rod, he traced a line across her belly then down to her pussy where he stopped and tapped the rod against her puffy flesh. He moved the tip to her thighs, then raised it upward again to her stomach.

The woman watched the rod travel over her body, but she never looked at Hoyte himself. Her muscles tensed and twitched as the rod traversed her oil-slicked skin. I think my muscles twitched as well.

Hoyte said nothing, gave no warning. He simply pulled back his arm and with a quick flick of his wrist, delivered a cracking blow across the woman's stomach.

She cried out.

Hoyte unleashed another strike across her stomach. Then another. Then he moved to her thighs. Crack! Crack! Crack. The helpless woman shuddered in her restraints and cried out, her big breasts shaking from the onslaught. Blows fell on her stomach and thighs, quick, sharp and relentless.

I could hear my heart beating in my ears. I could feel Michael's heart beating faster now, too, his excitement growing.

Hoyte stopped striking the woman. With his free hand he caressed the areas he'd struck. Thin red lines crisscrossed her stomach and thighs. He rubbed those lines and massaged her hurts until she began a low moan, then he reached between her legs and slid his fingers inside her slit.

Up and down he slid his fingers from her clitoris downward and back up again. He rubbed her and her moans grew louder and she began struggling in her restraints for a wholly different reason than before.

I, too, began to moan. Michael pinched and stroked me during the entirety of Hoyte's assault on the bound woman.

Once, Michael whispered to me, "This is nothing to what she's feeling. Nothing."

I couldn't stop staring at the red marks on the woman's stomach and thighs, fascinated by the evidence of coldly-delivered pain. Hoyte hadn't spoken a word to her during the storm of blows.

Hoyte stepped back and traced more lines with the tip of his rod, invisible lines across the woman's breasts. He prodded a nipple, then drew a trail across the undersides of her breasts.

The woman's moans of pleasure changed in tenor. They got louder, raising in pitch ... from fear, I knew, believing it could be nothing but that. Fear of what would come next. My palms grew sweaty and slick on the bar. I hadn't thought he might ... no ... not there ...

Hoyte pulled back his arm and delivered a cruel blow across the tops of her breasts. A terrible, shrill scream exploded from the woman. I barely had time to gasp before Hoyte struck again, this time claiming the undercurve of her breasts.

Her screams were frightful, loud, high-pitched and beyond anything I'd heard before. She continued to keen when Hoyte reached out to massage her poor flesh.

I couldn't look anymore. I closed my eyes and turned my head away. Surely a pain of that magnitude ... surely Hoyte couldn't rub it away. In my natural recoil from the scene, I released the bar and grabbed Michael's wrists. I fiercely held on to him, wanting everything to stop. It was too much for me. I wanted no more of it.

Michael yanked my hands off his wrists and with one hand, while with the other hand, he drove two fingers inside my pussy. I was so surprised, I didn't know what to do or think.

His voice was ominous. "I told you not to let go of that bar."

With each word he spoke, he plunged his fingers inside me. "Now ... grab ... the ... bar!"

He released my hands and I grabbed the bar. There was no way for me not to grab the bar.

"Watch them," he commanded.

And so I did. I watched Hoyte beat that poor woman's breasts, and I nearly cried along with her, but for different reasons. Michael's fingers worked a rhythm inside me, and when he stopped that, he tortured my breasts and nipples with fierce squeezes and pinches.

He pulled my nipples out farther and farther, my breasts stretching into conical shapes. He pinched until I was gasping. Then he let go and my breasts snapped back into their normal shape, until he attacked again.

He pinched and squeezed my pussy lips, too, when he wasn't fucking me with his fingers. I writhed my ass around on the bench and couldn't have spread my legs wider had I tried.

His harsh breathing sounded in my ears, and blew hot and humid on my shoulders and neck, where he nibbled and kissed me. His excitement fueled my own.

All the while, Hoyte beat that poor woman's breasts, slowly and deliberately, not saying a word to her, no longer intermittently soothing her burning flesh. He would strike. She would scream. Then maybe a ten count would pass. Then another blow fell on her poor breasts. Tears drenched her cheeks and dripped onto her red striped breasts.

Then came the final blow. It was beyond brutal.

Hoyte struck, aiming at the center of her breasts, cutting across her areolae and nipples. The woman shrieked like never before. I moaned for her.

Then Hoyte went into motion, unshackling the woman from the rack. In a few quick movements he released the clips from her leather manacles. She slumped in his arms, and he easily picked her up and carried her limp form under one of his beefy arms.

Hoyte took her to a nearby table where she lay her on her back, her legs draping over the side. She continued to keen, tears flowing, and wrapped her arms around her chest, cradling her poor, red-striped breasts.

Hoyte unzipped his pants, and pulled out his cock, leaving his pants buttoned at the top. He was uncircumcised and all-around large like the rest of him. He barked at the woman to spread her legs, the first words he'd said to her as long as I'd been watching. She obeyed and he grabbed her hips and drove his dick into her with one mighty thrust.

I gasped for air while the woman cried out. Hoyte called his wife over and told her to restrain the woman's arms to the table legs. Elaine scrambled to obey. The beaten woman didn't resist, probably couldn't resist, I thought.

Hoyte seized her poor swollen breasts with both of his meaty paws, using them as something like purchase for his thrusting. His hands were vises. He pumped into her and she cried out, in pain or in what may have been the beginnings of pleasure. I couldn't know which.

Michael sighed behind me, an odd sound at this moment. "Hoyte never was a master of timing. Oh, she'll come, but she would have come harder if he had just waited a few minutes longer, just a few more strokes."

He sighed again. "Oh well. So be it."

He gave my nipples a hard pinch, and then he got up. The air felt cold against my back when he left.

He stood in front of me and told me to look at him. His blue eyes were lit with a cold flame. Whether his passion was for me, or for the beaten woman, didn't much matter. It was my turn, now, I knew it, and I was beyond ready for him. He had brought me close to orgasm multiple times, then backed away. So yes, beyond ready didn't quite cover it. I was on the verge of pleading for release.

He unzipped his jeans, and like Hoyte, pulled out his cock without actually removing his pants. Michael's dick was circumcised, and hard and you could practically see the blood pulsing through the veins running just under the smooth skin. I wanted to reach out and touch it.

He seemed to read my mind. "Don't let go of the bar."

I held on.

"Open wide," he said, and he held his cock out, directing it toward my mouth.

I opened and leaned forward. He guided his dick between my lips. I sucked him in farther.

He tasted clean and musky, the same way he smelled. He wrapped his hands around the back of my head, and it soon became clear that I was not, technically speaking, giving him a blow job. It was more like he was fucking my mouth.

He held my head firm and tight, while he pushed his dick deeper into my mouth, eventually bumping up against the back of my throat. I tried not to gag, and he pulled back. In a slow rhythm, he pushed himself back inside me.

He told me when he wanted me to suck, and when to suck harder, then softer. Sometimes he stopped and pulled out, then had me lick and kiss the length of his cock. Then he pushed it past my lips again, and thrust back inside me.

While Michael was fucking my mouth, the sounds of fucking continued in the room beyond the glass wall. Hoyte's baritone grunting and harsh breathing, the woman's higher-pitched moans and gasps of delight. More than once I heard what could have only been the smack of a hand on flesh. Good God, I thought, he still hasn't had done with her. I couldn't imagine how she could bear it.

In our own room, Michael's pace increased with the pace of the grunting in the other room. He pumped into me more ferociously than ever, his rapid breathing a quieter version of Hoyte's.

Michael's hands tightened around my head and his hips bucked, and I felt a rising alarm when it seemed I couldn't escape his thrusts even if I tried my hardest. His dick kept pushing deeper into my mouth, coming closer and closer to triggering my gag reflex.

He commanded that I suck harder, and so I did, and he pumped into me, over and over. Then at last, the woman beyond the glass wall orgasmed; the cries were unmistakable. Hoyte slapped and grunted, then he too cried out his release.

And Michael shoved into my mouth, hard, hitting the back of my throat, and I gagged violently, my body heaving. He pulled out, leaving me choking and coughing and holding back vomit. Some saliva spilled out of the sides of my mouth, dripped down to my breasts.

Michael rapidly stroked his dick up and down, his breath a pulsing beat in the air. Faster he went, and faster, until at last, he came, his climax marked by spurts of semen splatting on my breasts.

His eyes were hooded and half closed while he rubbed the tip of his deflating penis over my semen- and saliva-covered breasts. He blended the semen and saliva into a goo across my nipples and areolae.

The moans in the other room slowed and grew ever softer. I finally controlled my gagging, and my panic.

Then Michael leaned down behind me and picked up the remote control. With a few pushes, the sounds of breath and moans abruptly ceased, and the big white curtain rolled closed. The world suddenly became a much smaller place.

Michael tucked his cock back into his pants. He walked behind me. I simply sat there, my heart still beating hard from the combination of desire and panic. I waited, wondering what was coming next. In spite of what he'd done, how he had scared me, I still wanted him.

"You can let go. Come here," he said.

I gratefully released the accursed bar and wiped my sweaty palms on my thighs.

Michael pulled a towel out of a drawer that was hidden in the wall. He wetted it down with some bottled water he pulled from the mini-bar. With a firm hand, he cleaned the mess off my breasts.

He wiped his hands on a clean corner of the towel, then dropped it on the floor. He walked about picking up his clothes, sorting out his shirt and pulling it over his head. He gathered my things together, too, and brought them to me.

"Sorry about your shirt," he said. "It's pretty wrinkled. Guess we should have hung it up or something." Then he grinned, showing he wasn't actually all that sorry.

I didn't care about the stupid shirt. I had a larger issue at hand. I stared, practically open-mouthed, at the clothes he held out to me. Was I supposed to get dressed now? Was it over? Impossible. I was in need. It wasn't time to get dressed. What the hell?

Misreading my confusion, Michael said, "It's okay. Go ahead. Get dressed. We're done."

And I thought, "We're done?"

Since I wasn't taking the clothes, Michael shrugged and dropped them onto the seat of the recliner. He strolled over to the mini bar, where he rummaged around then pulled out a can of soda. He popped the top and took a long, and apparently, satisfying drink.

It was the smug satisfaction on his face that finally helped me find my voice.

What I said next sounded more a statement than a question. "What the hell do you mean by that? We're done? I'm not done."

"Oh, I'm sorry. I don't mean we're done forever. I just meant we're done for the night."

"But I'm not done. I feel ... I need ..." I didn't want to have to ask for it, but I decided it wouldn't kill me to set my pride aside for the moment, not if it got me what I wanted. And maybe he wanted me to ask for it.

"I need you," I told him. "Don't leave me hanging." There, I'd said it.

Michael laughed. He laughed at me. Not a big laugh, but big enough and long enough to tell me that leaving me hanging was exactly what he planned to do.

I gaped at him. It's not that I consider myself to be some irresistible specimen of womanhood. Far from it, in fact. I have insecurities, same as anyone else. But really, his response had gone too far. I knew the man wanted me. For God's sake. A moron would know he wanted me.

Finally after a few aborted sputters, I let my true feelings be known. "Well, this is a big bunch of bullshit."

He laughed again. An evil glint in his eyes told me he knew I was frustrated and he didn't care. "It's not bullshit. It's your punishment. Don't you remember? I think it happened when Hoyte laid his rod across that woman's breasts."

He paused for a moment, watched my face. I had no idea what he was talking about.

He clarified. "You let go of the bar."

I said nothing. I remembered. That's right. I had let go of the bar. Only for a moment. It had been a natural response, my wanting to pull away. It was nothing. An accident. I hadn't thought of it again. Besides, later I'd held onto that bar when I desperately wanted to let go. That should count for something.

"I told you not to disobey me a third time," he said. "I warned you the repercussions would be severe."

My desire for the man had been fading from the moment he laughed at me, and now whatever remained of that desire was completely wiped away, replaced with swelling anger.

My words were snappish, punctuated with reproach. "So, since I let go of the bar for a few seconds, out of shock, I might add, not because I was deliberately disobeying you, my punishment is that I don't get fucked."

"Well," he said, "one could say that you did get fucked tonight, just not the way you wanted. The actual punishment is that you don't get to orgasm. No coming for you."

"And what's to stop me from masturbating right now, until I come?"

Without missing a beat he said, "I am." And he said it so softly and powerfully, that without a doubt, I knew he could and would stop me.

It was the change of tone in his voice that reminded me I was standing there in front of him wearing only high heels and a pair of panties. The realization only made me angrier.

I reached down and snatched up my clothes. In a rush, I yanked on the rumpled items. I wanted out of that room and away from that man. I was angrier than I'd been in a long time.

Michael leaned casually against the wall, looking again like a bored playboy. He sipped his drink and watched me with that damnable smug smile. He was between me and the door.

Where the hell was my purse? Oh, there it was, on the table right in front of Michael. Of course it was.

I snatched it up and was sailing past him when he reached out an arm and scooped me in next to him. I fought his grasp for only a moment. There was no point fighting him. I gave up and stared at the door and seethed.

"Let me go," I said.

"I will, in a moment. But first hear me out. Will you hear me out?"

I didn't want to, not really. I said yes, though, since to do otherwise might have made me seem peevish. I'd be damned before I'd give him an excuse to call me peevish.

"When you came in here," he said, "you made an agreement with me that you'd do what I asked of you. Whether accidentally or not, you broke that agreement and you have to be punished for it. That's just how it is."

He waited a few moments then continued, "Next time we meet, you'll be more careful, because you'll remember this night and you'll try harder to obey me and to avoid any more accidents. In spite of your disobedience, I was pleased with you tonight. I think anyone would have been. So I have an offer for you."

I looked up into his wolf eyes for the first time since he grabbed me. "I'm not exactly feeling open to offers right now, especially not from you."

"That's okay. Just hear me out. Some people would call it an offer of training, but I don't call it that. Training sounds formal and ropes you in for the long haul. What I propose is that we commit to spending five nights together, exploring your limits and finding out more of what you don't yet know about yourself."

"Not a chance."

"You're angry. I'm okay with that. But think it over once you've calmed down later tonight, or tomorrow. Whenever. Here's my card."

He let go of me, then pulled a white card from his shirt pocket, opened my purse and dropped the card inside. "Call me if you decide to accept my offer. Five nights of discovery ... and passion."

"Unless I accidentally disobey," I said.

He only smiled, then he opened the door for me and guided me back down the hall. When we were in the main hall, he stopped outside a different door, a ladies restroom, and told me he'd wait while I freshened myself up. I told him not to bother, but after glancing at his face, I knew he would wait, regardless of my wishes.

I marched into the bathroom and when the door swung closed behind me, I took a long shaky breath. I didn't know about freshening up, but I damned well needed to get myself together.

"I think I hate him," I said out loud.

I started at the sound of a woman's gentle laugh.

« CHAPTER 6 »

ONE OF THE STALL DOORS swung open and out stepped Elaine Hoyte. She glanced at me before heading to a sink.

She washed her hands. "If only I had a nickel for every time I heard a woman say she hated a man in this place, or one for when she said she loved him." She shook her head, smiling at her own joke.

She pulled a few paper towels from the dispenser. "I'd have a nice stash of spending money just from Michael's ladies alone. That was you with him, wasn't it? Michael Weston?"

"Yeah, how'd you know that?"

"I try to obey my master in all things, when we're in a scene, but I can't help myself. Sometimes I peek around to see who's watching."

"And you saw me, with Michael."

"Sure. I know I shouldn't and I'll probably confess later tonight. I always do but ... hey, are you okay?"

I covered my face with my hands. "No, I'm not okay. I'm a moron."

"Look honey, being with that man doesn't make you a moron. He's all hell-a good lookin' and I've appreciated a chance or two to scene with him."

I dropped my hands and stalked to the mirror. There I was. Looked the same. I began the evening thinking I was a fairly intelligent person, now I found out that I had the brain of a lemur. Or a lemming. Yeah, more like a stupid, stupid lemming.

"No, I didn't mean Michael," I said. "Although, I'm beginning to wonder. Do you know what I thought? I can't believe it. I'm an idiot."

Elaine's expression was both kind and bemused.

I wanted to smack my forehead. "I didn't realize that big window went both ways. I mean, I guess I didn't think about it. I thought it was like one of those mirrors in cop shows, when a witness ID's a suspect, you know. A one-way mirror, where you can see, but not be seen. That's what I thought."

Elaine started to laugh, I think, but took pity on me and stopped herself. "Aw, honey, don't worry about it. Doesn't make any difference anyway. My husband and me, we've just about seen it all. You and Michael weren't doing anything in there that was worth tellin' tales about."

I covered my face with my hands again.

Elaine tsked-tsked then came over and patted me on the shoulder. "That didn't come out right. I meant you don't need to be embarrassed. Ron and I wouldn't ever say anything to anyone about you. It's the code around here. It's meant to be safe."

I blew out a loud breath and uncovered my face. There I was. Still in that damned mirror. Dumb as a rock. Pity.

Elaine asked if I had a brush in my purse. She pulled it out and ran it through my hair, setting me to rights, as she put it, saying it would make me feel better. Then she gently wiped away a few smudges of mascara from under my eyes, and rummaged around in my purse to find my lip gloss which I managed to apply without giving myself a cerebral hemorrhage from overworking my barely-flickering brain cells.

When we were done, Elaine was proved correct. I actually did feel better. At least, I felt good enough to get the hell out of the club with whatever scrap of dignity I had left.

Elaine gave me a motherly pat on my arm. "I'm Elaine Hoyte, by the way."

I told her that I knew her name because of Michael, then I introduced myself in return.

"Look, Nonnie," she said, "I can tell you're new. And Michael's just the man for someone who's new."

She ignored my grunt, and continued. "But that doesn't mean you couldn't use a woman's help, too. I'll give you my number, so if you have any questions, or just want to talk, you can give me a call. We'll have coffee or somethin'."

At the moment, I couldn't imagine pursuing this new interest any further, but Elaine had been kind to me, so I returned her smile and entered her number into my cell phone.

"Um," I said, "I'd appreciate it if you wouldn't tell Michael about, you know."

"Oh, honey, he won't care that you said you hate him. He'd probably like it."

"No, not that. But yeah, don't tell him that either, not if he'd like it. What I meant was, don't tell him about me thinking the glass wall was a mirror. It's just too embarrassing."

"Done deal. Those men don't need to know everything, even if they think they do. Speaking of which, I'd best get back to my man. I've been gone too long and there's gonna be hell to pay."

She didn't appear worried about the bill. She looked pleased, in fact.

It made me think about another woman, and whether or not she had been pleased to pay Ron Hoyte's bill.

I risked the question. "Um, I hope it's okay to ask. That other woman in the room with you. Is she ... is she okay?"

Elaine's grin only got wider. "Okay wouldn't be the word for it. She's into pain, and the only complaint she's likely to have right now is that Ron didn't beat her long enough."

I shook my head, not because I didn't believe Elaine, but because I couldn't believe anyone would want more of what Ron had done.

Elaine shrugged. "Everybody's different, honey. I'm not into heavy duty pain myself, but gals like her are handy to have around when your husband's got an itch you're not up to scratching."

I couldn't help myself. It was the way she said it, so matter-of-fact, so blasé. I laughed.

She smiled. "I like you. You be sure to call." Then she headed to the door, asking one last time if I was okay.

I assured her I was, thanked her for her help and told her to go on.

Once she was gone, I used the toilet, spent a few more moments fiddling around in front of the mirror, then called a cab to come pick me up.

Michael was, as I anticipated, still waiting for me in the hall. His hair looked a bit damp, and I deduced that he had taken a few moments to freshen up in the men's room. I had a vision of him bent over the sink, splashing his face with water, a few drops landing on his hair, and him running his fingers through it, those strong fingers of his.

Enough of this, I told myself. Stop. He's nothing more than a good-looking ... good-looking ... asshole, I decided.

He held out a hand to me, but I shook my head. I didn't want to seem spiteful, but I simply didn't want to touch him. Or for him to touch me.

He didn't comment, and we walked down the halls side by side. He dropped the key card on Sarah's desk as we passed, Michael only briefly nodding in reply to her subservient, "Thank you, Sir."

When we rounded the corner to the last hall, Michael stopped. "Before we go out there, I want to tell you that I enjoyed myself very much tonight."

I mumbled a deliberately unintelligible nothing.

Michael wasn't fazed. "I'm hoping you'll take me up on my offer. I only ask that when you think about it, you remember what happened between us tonight, what happened before you had to be punished, and how you felt. I can make you feel that way again. And much, much more. Remember that."

I didn't say anything. He said I had to be punished. Had to. As if it were beyond his control, as if he didn't have a choice. I gritted my teeth.

We walked down the hall and out into the overblown blast of loud music and the clamor of the crowd.

Michael asked me to sit with him, to have another drink, whatever. I told him no, that I was leaving. He offered to wait outside with me for a taxi, but happily, at that moment, I spotted Lilly heading toward the door. I told him I'd catch a ride with her.

I'd be fine, I said, and no I didn't want him to come outside with me.

I wanted away from this place, from him.

He let me go.

When I reached the door, something made me glance back at him, to see what he was doing. There he was, standing where I left him. His stance was relaxed, his arms hanging loosely at his sides. But his expression was fierce, his mouth a straight line of intensity. When I met those pale blue eyes of his, he smiled a slow, half smile.

I turned away and left him behind.

I caught Lilly out on the sidewalk, but she wasn't alone. A nice-looking young man was chatting with her.

We exchanged hellos and I asked Lilly if she was getting a cab to return to the other bar. I left my car there, and assumed she'd done the same.

"No," Lilly said. "A friend dropped me off. Anyway, Scott and I have plans for a nightcap at his place, and his car is here."

They wanted to wait for my cab with me, but I told them to go. When I called from the ladies room, the dispatcher told me a car would be there in less than ten minutes, so I wouldn't have long to wait. It wasn't like I was alone. Although it was late, people steadily filtered in and out of the club.

Before they left, Lilly whispered to me that Scott was a definite trade-up from the man who stood her up at the restaurant earlier in the evening. I hoped she was right. We exchanged phone numbers, and they left.

I enjoyed the chance to take a few deep breaths, to wind down from the emotions of the evening. My anger with Michael wasn't as sharp as it had been. I hadn't forgiven him, certainly not, but at least I felt calmer, more myself.

I had just checked the time on my cell phone when a shiny black town car pulled up in front of the building. The rear window rolled down. I couldn't see inside the car, only a vague masculine outline. An arm appeared and waved me over.

I was reminded of hookers in television shows and movies. They were always being beckoned over to vehicles. The hookers would totter on their too-high heels, their round asses jiggling out of their, for lack of a better descriptor, skirts. More like half-skirts, really. They'd lean down and rest their crossed arms on the door, all the better for the johns to ogle their big boobies, my dear.

I grimaced. Some man in that town car probably thought I was a hooker. What a jerk. I might have been loitering around in front of a sex club, but my skirt was way too long for me to be a streetwalker. Okay, so maybe it was true that less than a half hour ago, I'd given a man a blow job in front of other people. What did that make me?

Not a hooker, I thought. And I motioned at the man in the car to go away.

He leaned out of the window so I could see him. I blinked when I recognized his face. The Businessman.

The Businessman. Again. Tonight. Curious.

I couldn't imagine what he wanted. I couldn't resist finding out.

I walked over to the car, not tottering in the slightest.

"Can I give you a ride home?" he asked with a friendly smile. "It's probably not safe for you out here."

"I'm waiting for a cab."

"I'm here right now. And I won't charge you the way a cab will."

I leaned forward and looked into the car, mentally shaking myself for being unable to block another vision of those hookers.

The Businessman was alone in the back seat. In the front, behind the steering wheel, sat a man wearing a suit, obviously the driver.

I thought, what the hell. I still had a desire to know The Businessman better, to know him at all. If I said no, I might never see him again.

He opened his door and I got in the car.

I slid into the back seat. The interior was all black leather and dark wood accents. It smelled of new car, the leather itself, and a hint of The Businessman's spicy scent. I well-remembered that spice.

I gave the address of the bar to the driver, then The Businessman pressed a button on an instrument panel, raising a smoky glass divider between us and the front seat. Though the interior of the town car was not as large as that of a limousine, the back seat area was still lengthy enough to retain the feel of spaciousness.

"That address sounds familiar," The Businessman said.

"It's a bar, the bar, where we met. I left my car there earlier." I tried not to sound awkward, failed all the same.

He looked sharp, put together, fit in a midnight blue shirt tucked into dark grey trousers. I wondered why I hadn't noticed what he was wearing when I saw him earlier in the evening. Oh, yeah, because I'd been too busy noticing how pissed off he was.

Illumination from passing street lights and the glow of the instrument panel provided enough light to see with some clarity. I looked at The Businessman. He wasn't angry anymore. He appeared convivial in the role of host and benefactor of free rides.

"Ah, of course. I certainly remember that bar, and that night," he said.

Free ride, I thought, wincing at the double entendre, and looked away.

He surprised me then. "I've thought of that night more than once in the last week. Have you?"

Well yes, I had, I might have answered. Only thought and thought about it so many times that I came out tonight looking for you, and somehow, in the course of the evening, wound up being fucked over by a hot guy I just met. And, oh yeah, I'm probably an exhibitionist. And a moron. Don't forget the moron part.

I settled on a simpler answer. "Yes."

"Good," he said.

There was something about this man. He said the word "good" and I felt a tiny burst of what I can only describe as happiness. Good. And I was happy.

The emotion was short-lived, gone with his next question. "How long have you known Michael Weston?"

"We just met, tonight," I answered.

"At Private Residence?"

At what? Oh, I remembered. That was the name of the sex club. "Yeah."

"I see. Are you in the habit of letting strangers fondle you in public?"

"What?" The man certainly had a way with the blunt questions. "That's none of your business."

"I didn't mean to offend you. It was an honest question. I was looking for an honest answer. That's all."

He sounded so reasonable, I distrusted my initial response. He'd seen me with Michael, Michael's hand in my bra, in public. The Businessman himself had been with me in a public hallway, my ass bare, and me panting when he talked of someone seeing us there. If he came to certain conclusions based on those facts, well I could hardly be offended by a logical assessment of my actions.

"No," I said, "I'm not in the habit of letting strangers fondle me in public."

"I thought as much," was his only reply.

Well, I thought, that was reassuring, though why it was reassuring, I wasn't sure. Because he didn't think I was a slut? No, I didn't think that was it. Besides, for all I knew, he might prefer slutty women.

We rode in silence for a minute or two. I wondered why I thought about being a slut, and how closed-minded that made me feel of a sudden.

"Has Weston made you an offer of training?" he asked.

And the surprises just kept coming. "Kind of, yes. I guess. I don't see how you could know that. Have you got me bugged or something?"

That earned a smile from him. "No. It's only that you're an attractive young woman. There's something of a ... a promise in you. Weston would see that, too. So of course he made you an offer. Have you accepted?"

"No. He asked me to think about it."

Was that a twitch of a muscle in The Businessman's strong jawline? Impossible.

"I don't like to speak poorly of others, but I want to give you something of a warning about him. If you accept his offer, be careful," he said.

"Be careful. What do you mean?"

"Guard yourself. Protect your interests. It's not my place to say more. However, you might consider asking others about him and his history. That's up to you."

It wasn't much of an answer. Its clarity ranked up there with what Michael had said about him, that he was unfeeling to the women under his care.

"Michael told me a rumor about you," I said.

"Did he?" His tone was bland, unconcerned. "You don't need to share it with me. I'm sure that whatever he told you, it's not flattering."

It wasn't necessary to tell him he was correct. The way he spoke of Michael, I had to believe that Michael had understated the level of their acquaintance.

"Before you make a decision about Weston's offer, I'd like to meet with you, privately, intimately," The Businessman said.

I stared at him.

He continued. "I might have a counteroffer, so to speak, for you."

My stomach muscles tightened of their own will, and my mouth went dry. I didn't know what to say, so I nodded a tell-me-more nod.

"A few hours, Monday evening," he said.

I nodded again.

The car pulled to a stop. We had arrived at the bar. That was fast, I thought. Everything was fast these days.

"So, will you meet with me, Monday evening?" he asked.

"Yes," I answered, then blinked. The answer had flown out of my mouth without any true consideration on my part. No chance to take it back.

He asked me what time I got off work on Monday, then told me to leave work and go straight to the Frederick Hotel. I assured him I knew the location of the Frederick.

He told me to give my name at the front desk and I would be shown to my room. I was not to tip anyone; he would take care of that. I didn't need to bring anything, either. He would provide everything I might need.

He then said he might be a little late, depending on a meeting he had to attend, but that I should be confident he would be there as soon as he could.

Before I got out of the car, he joked about the ride being so short he doubted he'd saved me much money. Then he gave me one of his chaste goodbye kisses, on my cheek this time.

But his final words weren't polite.

He looked at me, straight and even, his voice deep and low. "You smell of him. I don't like it."

Then I was climbing out of his car, almost as if he psychically willed me onto the street. And I was walking to my car, getting in and starting the engine. I noticed that The Businessman didn't leave until I pulled away down the street.

I drove home wondering about him and how easily I fell in line with his wishes. I hadn't even seriously considered declining his invitation of a ride, nor his invitation to meet with him again.

Maybe, some time before I went to the bar the night of my divorce celebration, someone had nabbed me and hypnotized me, then told me to go out and have kinky encounters with strangers who wanted to order me around. An unlikely scenario, perhaps.

The most likely answer for my recent behavior was that I was finally going after something I always wanted, but never knew I wanted it, or didn't want to face accepting it.

I didn't know. It had been a long night.

When I was home, freshly showered and tucked in bed, ready for sleep, I mentally relived a montage of my time with Michael, the Hoytes, and the girl on the rack.

But my last thoughts, before I drifted off to sleep, were of The Businessman, and the heat in his dark eyes — the way he looked when he saw me with Michael. And the way he looked when he said he didn't like the smell of another man on me.

And I thought, I still don't know his name.

« CHAPTER 7 »

THE BELLBOY QUIETLY SHUT the door of room 1032, leaving me alone.

Everything went as The Businessman said it would. I gave my name at the front desk and was immediately escorted to my room. Everyone was courteous, discreet.

I had no idea how The Businessman knew my name. I knew he never asked me. It was one of several mysteries I wished solved. Between the questions and the anticipation of seeing him again, I was wired for sound, as an old friend used to say.

Sunday afternoon I surfed the Internet, reading about BDSM and looking at pictures, pictures of women and men, bound and tortured. I scanned through pages describing Doms and subs, Masters and Mistresses and slaves, and contracts and training and on and on and on, the content jumbling together in short order.

It was the pictures, the damned pictures. They freaked me out, plain and simple. Some of the things that were being done to the people in the pictures ... I didn't even want to think about it. I had to stop looking.

Had I continued with my research, I don't think I would have been standing in that hotel suite. I pushed what I read and the accompanying pictures to the back of my mind, shoved it all behind my mind's image of the heady and handsome Businessman.

The Frederick Hotel was one of the oldest and finest hotels in the city. I'd never stayed there before, though I had splurged a few times and eaten in the restaurant.

Room 1032 was a small suite, comprised of a bedroom, a huge bathroom, and a sitting/dining room. A pair of French doors opened onto a terrace. The rooms had high ceilings and were loaded with heavy brocades, plush carpets and gold fixtures.

The furnishings were made from a dark and rich-looking wood, the rich part explaining why I had no idea what kind of wood it was. Everything shone from decades of polish and care. One piece in the bedroom, a free-standing mirror, caught my eye because of its obvious age and the beveled, oval glass that shone pristine and unclouded, belying its years.

As I toured the place, I noticed the scent of flowers, and not just from the fresh ones which were artfully placed about the rooms. There was an addition of jasmine, I thought, and orange blossoms.

I ended my tour back where I started, in the sitting room, and dropped my purse on the coffee table. I noticed an envelope with my name on it. I opened it and read the note inside.

The strong lines of a masculine hand slanted across the page:

"I hope the accommodations are to your liking. Help yourself to anything you would like to eat or drink. Please limit yourself to no more than one alcoholic beverage.

"Before I arrive, shower and wash your hair with the toiletries I've provided. Remove all makeup. Dry your hair, but don't style it or add hair products. When you've done this, you may wear one of the bathrobes that are hanging in the bathroom. Wear nothing else.

"I should be there before seven. Do what I tell you to do, and all will be fine."

It was signed, "Best," then a scrawl for the name. Damn. No matter how hard I tried, I couldn't make out the name. There was nothing to make out, just a big loop thing and a short squiggly line.

I reread the note. Then I read it again. So, this was how it was.

I assumed he didn't want me to drink too much for the same reason as Michael. I was fine with that, not being a big drinker anyway. Besides, I knew this wasn't going to be a normal kind of encounter. He would make demands of me, and wasn't that why I was here?

The Businessman wasn't asking much of me in his note. I didn't even mind not styling my hair. But no makeup? Really? Not even a touch of mascara, I presumed. I wasn't thrilled about that command, and couldn't imagine the point of the prohibition.

I was to do what he told me to do. Every time I heard that sort of thing I would get the mixed reactions of excitement and distrust. Excited to do what he wanted. Distrustful because … because I'm not a mindless person with no will of her own.

What did it say of me that I wanted to give that will to another? My distrust was not for The Businessman, or Michael. It was me I distrusted, me and these new desires. I didn't understand them in the least.

I checked the clock hanging over the bar in the back corner of the room. A little after six. I had plenty of time, but figured I might as well get started. I grabbed a cola out of the mini-fridge on my way to the bathroom.

It wound up taking longer than I thought it would. It was the shower's fault; there were all these water jets set into the walls, giving me a hell of a full-bodied massage. Bliss.

I found soap and shampoo sitting neatly on a shelf. According to the plain black print on the white containers, the products were hypo-allergenic and unscented. There was nothing else on the tubes and jars, no name brand, nothing. It was the same with the antiperspirant he provided, and the lotion I rubbed into my skin when I finished showering.

I quickly checked myself in the mirror. My hair was clean and shiny, hanging down my back, but it didn't look right, just hanging there all plain. I thought my face looked plain, too, undefined and dull without make-up. I briefly considered pinching my cheeks and lips, the way I recalled heroines doing in the historical romance novels I read when I was a teenager. I didn't bother. If he wanted me plain like this, then that's what he would get.

I wrapped myself in the luxurious white bathrobe that hung on the bathroom door then headed back to the sitting room.

I glanced at the clock. Ten until seven. My stomach fluttered. He would be here any time. I sat down on the sofa to wait. Maybe some TV would help me relax. No. No TV. I waited.

A few minutes later, there was a solid knock on the door, making my nerves jump, and then the knob turned. The Businessman walked in, looking more businessman-like than ever. He wore a dark blue suit that perfectly fit his tall, muscular figure. His shirt was crisp, white and fresh, as if he hadn't been wearing it all day. A shiny silk tie was snugged around his neck.

This was the first time I'd seen him in full light. He was as handsome as ever, with his fine Roman nose and his dark hair brushed back from his forehead, though I noticed some strands of silver hair around his temples. They only added to his attractions.

And his lips. He smiled at me, sitting there on the sofa. Me, looking plain and feeling small, wrapped up in the big, thick bathrobe. I smiled a shaky smile and stood.

He closed the door. "You should have thrown the deadbolt. It's more secure than the doorknob lock."

I thought, great, his first words to me are a safety lesson.

He turned the deadbolt then walked over to me.

"You're right, I didn't think about it," I said.

"Just remember." He reached out and cupped my jaw, turning my head to one side and then the other. "You found my note."

I nodded.

"You did everything I asked you to do?"

I told him I did.

"Good." He walked off toward the bar.

I stood there and waited, enjoying my good girl tingle, while he pulled a bottle of sparkling water from the fridge. He poured some water into a glass, nabbed one of the small bags of nuts on the bartop, then returned to the sitting area.

"Have you had plenty to drink? Are you hungry?" he asked, unbuttoning his suit jacket and sitting down in one of the big cushioned chairs.

"Yes, and no, not hungry."

"I meant to grab a snack on my way over here, but didn't get a chance." He tore open the bag and ate some of the nuts.

I stood there, feeling awkward, not knowing if I should sit or what.

He loosened his tie and unbuttoned the top few buttons of his shirt, reminding me of how he looked the first time I saw him, sans tie, of course. He casually lifted one of his legs and propped his ankle on his other knee, the male version of crossed legs, or that's how I always thought of it.

"Take off the robe and leave it on the sofa, then stand over here." He pointed to the floor, about five or six feet in front of his chair.

He ate another handful of nuts and chased it with some water. I stood there and stared at him, watching the muscles work in his jaw while he chewed. Just like that? Get naked? In all this light? No seduction, no soft candlelight, no kiss ... just get naked. It was so ... business-like.

Look who you're with, I thought, and almost laughed. God, I was nervous. Of course it was businesslike. I ordered myself not to go all giddy.

While I was thinking these thoughts, The Businessman observed me with an unflappable expression.

"Obviously, I need to explain a few things," he said. "First, you don't need to think about anything, not really. Just do what I tell you to do. Second, should you not want to do what I tell you, simply let me know, and you'll be free to leave. That's all. Two things. Easy, right?"

I thought, not really, but I said yes.

"So then ..." he continued, and let silence stretch behind his words, leaving what was unspoken to hang between us, only making the slightest of gestures toward the spot on the carpet, the spot where I was supposed to stand, naked.

He finished his snack while I reached for the tie of the robe. Time to do what I was told to do. And it was nowhere near as easy as he said.

I slipped off the robe, laid it on the sofa then went to where I was told to stand. He sipped his water and slowly perused me, top to bottom. He told me to turn. I turned. He told me to stop. I stopped. Even with my back turned, I felt his gaze on me. I looked over my shoulder and found him studying my ass.

Embarrassed. I was embarrassed. And turned on, too, or at least getting that way. I don't know how I could have stood there naked in front of him and not have gotten aroused. I would have been more excited, however, if I could have figured out what he was thinking, if he approved of what he saw.

Once I faced him again, he continued with the orders. "Clasp your hands behind your back. No, down low."

He told me to pull my shoulders back, then to spread my feet about shoulder-width apart. He had me lift my chin, straighten my legs, suck in my stomach, look at the floor.

"This is the attention stance. When I tell you to wait at attention, this is what I expect," he said.

I nodded.

"When you're standing at attention, you may not move or speak or look at anything other than the floor, unless I tell you to do so. Do you understand? Speak."

"Yes."

He left me standing there in that pose while he sipped his water and studied me. I thought of Michael's position number one.

I didn't want to be thinking of Michael. Although my anger toward him had cooled considerably, now was not the time to think of him. If The Businessman knew I was thinking of Michael, what would he do? Best not to find out.

"Clasp your hands on top of your head and stick your ass out more," he said.

I did.

"That's the first inspection stance. Do you understand? Speak."

I told him yes.

"Now spread your legs wider and bend over. Try to touch the floor. Good. Try to put your palms flat on the floor. Not quite there, huh? No matter, it can give you something to work on. Go as far down as you can. There. Now raise your head as far as you can, but keep your focus on the floor. Good. That's the second inspection stance. Do you understand? Speak."

"Yes."

He told me to stand closer, only about a foot or so in front of him, then he had me repeat the attention stance, and then the first inspection, which he had me hold.

"I like the way you've trimmed your pubic hair," he said. "I prefer the labia be completely bare, the way you've done yours. And the triangle of hair above your clitoris is fine, though I'd rather you trim it shorter, maybe a quarter of an inch more."

I thought to myself that apparently nothing was beneath his notice, not even the length of my pubic hair. It was disconcerting, and fascinating.

He wasn't finished disconcerting me. "Are you currently using some form of birth control?"

"Yes."

"Do you have any STD's that you're aware of?"

"No."

"Are you willing to be tested for STD's and other communicable diseases?"

"I guess, yes."

"Good. The boring questions are out of the way. Now, have you ever been tied up, for real, in a bondage sense, other than the night we were together?"

I answered no.

"Have you ever been whipped, or struck with a cane or paddle?"

I didn't think a few swats from Michael's belt counted as any of those, so I answered no.

"Spanking? Other than the minor one I gave you."

I answered no, but wondered at him deeming it minor. It seemed like a pretty major spanking to me at the time.

He asked me more questions about my sexual history, such as if I had ever had sex with a woman, if I had ever had sex with more than one man at the same time, if I had ever participated in an orgy, if I had ever been filmed while having sex. No, no, no. Always, the answer was no.

I wouldn't have thought it possible to be standing naked, posed no less, in front of a fully-dressed man, and yet feel that I was guilty of having a tame sex life.

His next question truly surprised me. "You were in one of the viewing rooms at Private Residence Saturday night. What were they doing in the display room?"

I hesitated. How did he know? I thought he left the club after he saw me, obviously an incorrect assumption. It made me uncomfortable to think of him watching while I went into the VIP area with Michael.

"I watched a woman get beaten with a rod," I answered.

I wished I could see his reaction, because I suspected there was one. There was an edge to his voice when he asked, "How badly was she beaten?"

"I don't know. I mean, I've never seen anything like that before. It seemed really bad to me, but she was liking parts of it, the way he touched her after he hit her. She had all these red welts and I didn't want to watch anymore after he hit her breasts."

The sharp edge still remained in his tone. "So did you keep watching?"

"Yes,"

"Why?"

I took a breath. I couldn't avoid mention of Michael now. Let it be on The Businessman, though. I didn't control the questioning. "Because Michael made me."

"How did he make you? Were you restrained, unable to leave?"

"No. I could have left. He told me that. I guess, well ... there was this bar he made me hold and ... he just made me watch. I don't really ..." I floundered around. It was an excellent question, one I surprisingly couldn't answer.

The Businessman didn't say anything. He waited for a complete response. What was it? Was I afraid of punishment if I stopped watching? No, I wasn't thinking about punishments at that point. Michael hadn't threatened me. I remembered him shoving his fingers inside me and ordering me to grab the damnable bar. He told me to keep watching.

Finally, I said the only truth I knew, though it seemed lacking. "I guess he made me keep watching by telling me to do it."

The Businessman was silent for a while longer. Some of the edge was gone from his voice when he finally did speak. "Okay. Now turn around."

And I supposed that was that, at least for him. I wasn't going to forget the question, though. I believed there should be a better answer than the one I gave.

I turned around, holding the inspection pose.

"Second inspection stance," he said.

A few moments before that order, I didn't think it possible that I could be more embarrassed. I didn't want to bend over. Through all of the posing and questioning I never forgot how bright the room was, how naked I was, in every way. He still wore his jacket, for God's sake. And now I was supposed to bend over, right in front of him? I couldn't do it.

But I only had one other choice, to tell him I wouldn't do it, which meant putting on my clothes and leaving. I didn't want to leave. I needed a middle ground, a middle ground that he made clear didn't exist. Hell. I bent over.

I wished for some background noise in the room, music, or television, or even the ticking of an old-time clock, anything to break up The Businessman's silent study of my most private parts. Between the awkwardness of my full reveal and the blood rushing to my head because of the position, I knew my face was growing red, a certainty that only made everything worse.

His voice cut through my consternation. "Have you ever had anal intercourse?"

I may have said "Eep." I know I said, "God no."

"Okay. You can stand up straight. No position. We're going to the bedroom."

And then he stood up and headed off into the next room.

Naturally, I followed. But slowly. I wondered to myself if he were deliberately trying to shake me with his questions. What was his game? I couldn't be blamed for wondering. I didn't know how anyone could spend any amount of time with someone so shuttered, so closed off, and not wonder what he was thinking.

The way he looked me over, and the questions, it was like an interview, a naked, sexy interview, but one all the same.

I joined him in the bedroom and he instructed me to remove the bedspread and blanket from the king-sized bed and to pile them in a corner of the room. While I did that, he shrugged out of his jacket, removed his tie, and rolled up the sleeves of his shirt. I would have preferred he take off his shirt with the jacket, but it wasn't my call, was it? At least we were in the bedroom, a serious improvement over the sitting room.

He told me to climb into the center of the big bed. Then he explained he wanted me to "display" myself, his word, not mine. I knelt, similar to how Elaine Hoyte knelt on the floor of the room in the sex club, the exception being that The Businessman insisted I spread my knees. He demanded further adjustments, which I obeyed as best I could.

Finally, he was satisfied. I was on my knees, which were spread apart, and my hands rested on my upper thighs. The arch in my back thrust out my breasts, and I held my head high with my eyes cast downward.

He called this the relax stance, something of a misnomer in my opinion, since trying to hold the pose on the soft mattress was a serious study in maintaining balance.

I tried to keep steady while he went over to the antique, full-length mirror. The mirror's feet must have been on sliding casters, because he didn't even grunt when he pushed the massive piece of furniture toward the foot of the bed.

He maneuvered the mirror directly in front of me, then adjusted the tilt until my image was reflected dead center. He pulled one of the chairs over beside the mirror and sat down.

He casually crossed his legs. "Look at yourself."

I did. I thought dumbly, yep, that's me.

"Tell me three things you like about your body."

I couldn't resist glancing at him. Was he serious? He met my gaze. Yes, he was serious. Okay then. Three things I liked.

"Well, I guess my hair is all right, though it's not so great right now, kind of frizzy because I didn't style it."

"What do you like about your hair?"

"It's thick, and has some waves. I like that it's long. I like that it's so dark, black. I don't color it."

"I can tell."

I risked another glance at him to see if the statement was a criticism.

"It's good that you don't color it," he said. "What else do you like?"

I studied myself in the mirror. I wasn't accustomed to searching for what I liked about my body. I would have said I liked my eyes, but without mascara and some eyeliner, my eyes didn't seem up to snuff. Eyes were out.

"My nose is okay. It's not too big, anyway."

"Okay. One more."

"My answer is kind of dumb."

"Tell me anyway."

"My knees."

"Why?"

"Well, when they're bent like this, they're not all bony and pokey-looking the way some people's knees are. I like that they're smooth."

"You're right, you have attractive knees."

I smiled.

"Now tell me three things you don't like about your body," he said.

I thought, only three? I had a certain level of confidence in my body, but that didn't mean I wasn't aware that it could be better, way better. I was a pro at finding things I didn't like about myself.

I wished that my lips were fuller, that I had more defined cheekbones, that my neck were longer, that my arms were more graceful, that my feet were smaller. No matter how many sit-ups I did, I wished my stomach were more toned and my waist narrower. No matter how many different cleansers and over-priced creams I used, I wished my skin were clearer. I wanted thicker fingernails and prettier teeth. A firmer butt. An endless critique.

I could only pick three? And I had to tell them to a man who was silently observing me, kneeling and naked, with legs spread? He didn't need me to tell him what was wrong with me. I was certain he already had a complete mental catalog.

I picked out three things, choosing my teeth and neck and feet. I mumbled the reasons. The exercise was humbling, shaming. I didn't like it.

He didn't speak until I was finished. "You didn't say anything about the obviously sexual parts of your body, like your breasts or ass."

I didn't have anything to say to that, so I stared at the white sheets.

"I personally believe that every part of a woman's body is erotic. And I find your body particularly appealing," he said.

A rush of warmth flashed over me.

"I put you in that pose because I want to watch you touch yourself, intimately."

I inhaled. Were we done, finally, with the questions and answers? I was definitely ready to be done with them.

"Touch your breasts," he said.

Yep, we were done with the questions. I touched my breasts.

"Squeeze them, gently."

I squeezed.

"Watch yourself in the mirror. Don't look away."

I stared at my reflection. Everything about me seemed small. My embarrassment read clearly on my face, which surprised me, since I was trying hard to suppress it. My hands looked tiny and weak on my breasts, squeezing tentatively, clumsily. I couldn't see myself in that little woman.

"Stop," said The Businessman, "but don't look away from the mirror. Listen to me very carefully."

I did as he asked and nodded.

His voice reached me low and clear. "There's no place for shame in what we do together. I enjoy a certain amount of humility in you, and some embarrassment, but not shame. Never that. If I didn't find you physically attractive, I wouldn't be with you. Remember that."

"I didn't put you in front of that mirror to degrade or humiliate you," he said.

He waited a few moments before continuing, allowed me to take in his words. "Saturday night at the club you were watched. Afterward, you watched others. I suspect you've never watched yourself, though. And so I've put you in front of this mirror."

Again he paused to give me time to think. His words soothed away much of my self-consciousness. He found me attractive. I definitely found him attractive.

And he was right about me never watching myself. It hadn't ever occurred to me.

"But the most important point here, is that I want to watch you touch yourself," he said.

He seemed far away, before, in that chair of his, the cryptic line of his lips, the inscrutable dark eyes. My awareness of his actual nearness grew as he told me he wanted to watch me touch myself. He soon seemed to be practically sitting next to me in the bed.

The sensual tenor of his voice reached out and calmed me, drew at me, scattered my reserve and my shame.

"I want you to touch your breasts again," he said. "If it helps you, imagine your hands are mine, that I'm the one squeezing your breasts."

I touched myself again, my hands steadier, less clumsy. I imagined it was him touching me.

"Good. Run your fingers over your nipples. Play with them. I want to see them hard."

I did as he said, and watched in the mirror as my nipples stiffened under my touch.

"Squeeze them between your fingertips. Harder. Just until it hurts."

I obeyed and sucked in my breath at the moment of pain.

"Twist them."

I twisted.

"Harder."

I twisted harder, and flinched.

He told me to pull my nipples, to rub and squeeze my breasts. He wanted me to pull harder, to rub harder, so I did. I watched my hands rub my breasts in the mirror. His hands, I thought. Where I wanted his hands to be.

He ordered me to squeeze my breasts tightly, until my hand was a claw and the flesh of my breasts bulged between my fingers. I clenched my jaw and tightened my stomach against the sharp sensations.

I fell into the flow of his command.

My breasts were tingling and tight when he ordered me to touch my stomach, then to move lower, between my legs. He told me to rub my pussy, to lightly pinch my labia and spread them open, to reveal all of myself in the mirror. To reveal myself to him.

He said, look, look at yourself, and so I did.

I flicked at my clitoris on his command. Then because he wanted to see me do it, I slid my fingers into the folds of my pussy. I grew ever warmer under his gaze, his low voice guiding my explorations. And the demands kept coming, and I obeyed them all, having drifted into a sort of unquestioning mode, a place where everything made sense, and nothing but pleasure could follow, if I did what he told me to do.

Now, a sexy me looked back from the mirror. My eyes were hooded and distant. My hair spread around my shoulders in shiny black tendrils. My breasts were high and reddened from my handling. My pussy glistened from the moisture that evidenced my arousal.

And he watched me. I felt his eyes on me. I wanted him to see me.

The more he commanded and the more I obeyed, the sexier I became. I no longer remembered that I'd been embarrassed and scared.

He told me to stick one finger inside myself. Then another. I groaned. He had me spread open my labia with my other hand, the better for me to see, the better for him to see. My fingers moved inside, standing proxy for his fingers.

He told me to stay as I was, then he stood and walked over to the bureau. He opened a drawer and pulled out a small black bag. After he tossed the bag onto the bed beside me, he took the pillows from the head of the bed and stacked them behind me.

He returned to his chair and told me to change position, to lean back against the pillows and bend my knees, to spread my legs wide. In the mirror, I was a wanton wild thing, splayed, ready for whatever might come. Did he see it? The wildness?

He had me open the black bag, search out a mid-sized black dildo and a tube of lubricant. He instructed me to put some of the slippery liquid on the dildo. I did everything he asked.

"Now, hold yourself open with your other hand and slip the dildo inside you, slowly, slowly," he said.

I slid the latex toy into my pussy. I groaned. My muscles stretched easily to accept it. Keeping my eyes on the mirror, I was fascinated by the way the dildo slowly disappeared inside my body.

He ordered me to pull it back out, also slowly. Then back in. Then out. In. My hips rose slightly to meet my hand as I pushed the smooth dildo into my pussy.

All the while, I thought of him doing these things to me. And in a real way, it truly was his hands. Mine had become his, under his command. I would do his bidding. The understanding grew under the erotic slow rhythm he set.

I looked away from the mirror, a powerful need pushing me to seek him out, to discover what he thought. He wasn't looking at my face, of course. No, he stared at my pussy, watched me fuck myself with his toy.

On first glance, he was as dispassionate as ever, as if he were watching a mildly interesting television show. His breathing was slow and even, unlike my own, which got louder and faster with each passing moment. I searched for signs, any sign, that there was more behind his impassive gaze.

There ... his hair, always perfectly arranged, it had fallen a bit on one side. And there ... a subtle, recurring twitch in his jaw. Was his hand gripping the arm of the chair with unnecessary force, was there tension in his forearm?

I decided there was. I needed it, needed him to be moved, to prove his desire. These suppositions, the potentially phantom evidence, were all I'd get from him for now.

And then he told me to rub my clitoris. I stroked across my clit, then around and around, harder when he told me he wanted harder, faster when he wanted faster. The dildo slid in and out of me, moving in a slick and steady rhythm.

The pressure grew inside me, and when I clamped down, the pleasure spiraled outward. Faster. He said to rub my clit faster. Not the dildo, he said. Keep it slow. I want it slow, he said. Rub harder. Faster.

"I want to see you come," he said.

So I clamped down onto the dildo, and I worked my clit. I watched his eyes, his dark eyes, always watching my pussy, watching my fingers. Faster, he ordered.

And the pressure grew, and grew, until it finally burst. My orgasm flooded through me, and his eyes met mine. I rode the pleasure, rode the desire I wanted to see in those dark, dark eyes.

I held his gaze as my orgasm faded away into the diminishing repeated pulse of my clit. Then he broke our gaze and looked at my pussy. I turned my eyes to the mirror, to see what he saw.

I was sprawled, slack-limbed, looking satiated, for the moment. The dildo laid in my hand, loosely, more like it was resting there than being held. My labia were red and swollen. I appeared to be waiting. Not finished. Indeed, I felt far from finished.

I soon discovered I was alone in that feeling.

The Businessman smiled. "You did well. I enjoyed it. Thank you. Now, tidy yourself up, if you wish, but don't take too long. I'm expected somewhere else this evening. I'll be in the other room."

He stood, leaned down and patted my knee, then turned away. I flashed on Michael telling me we were done. Is that what The Businessman was doing? Was he telling me we were done?

He hadn't even touched me, except for that pat on my knee. I couldn't recall him touching me any other time. We couldn't be done.

And he said that he had somewhere to be. Did he actually say that?

I jerked myself upright. My disbelief and disgust tumbled out in sharp notes and edges. "Is this it? Is that what you're saying?"

« CHAPTER 8 »

HE TURNED BACK TO ME, an eyebrow arched in silent question.

"Basically, I'm dismissed," I said. "We're done here. Is that right?"

"Not exactly. There are a few things I want to discuss with you, but other than that, yes, I suppose we're finished."

"That's just great." I couldn't fail to notice that he didn't like the tone I was using with him, but in that moment, I didn't care. "You could at least tell me what stupid rule I broke. Let me guess, I looked away from the mirror, so I have to be punished."

"Why do you think you're being punished?"

"You've got to be kidding me." My voice grew louder as my outrage fueled the volume. "You're not going to have sex with me, and you ask why I think I'm being punished? It's unbelievable. After what I just did? You never even touched —"

I didn't get to finish my sentence. In two quick strides he was on the bed next to me. Before I could process what was happening, he grabbed me, flipped me onto my stomach, and pushed a knee into my lower back. With one hand, he restrained my wrists, arms bent at the elbow, my hands pressed against the middle of my back.

He weighed heavily on me, forcing me to work hard to breath. One side of my face was mashed into the mattress, but I could still see the mirror, see how I appeared crushed, flattened under his bulk. He loomed over and beside me, glowering, his leg in my back an immovable pillar.

I struggled, no matter the futility of it. I wanted away.

His question erupted as a growl. "Do you think this is a game I'm playing with you?"

I didn't answer and tried to pull out of his hold. Impossible.

"Maybe it's a game to you," he said, "but I assure you it's not, not to me. You speak to me as if I owe you something, as if you earned some reward that I've denied you, like I've cheated you."

I gulped air, my words a raspy plea. "Let me go."

"No problem. And then we're truly done. We'll part ways for good. Just say the word and I'll let you go."

I wanted to say it. I truly did. But I couldn't. I didn't know why, but I couldn't say it. I stopped struggling and tried to catch my breath.

"What is it? What did I fail to give you? What do you want?" he asked.

I didn't answer.

He delivered a resounding smack to my bare ass. "Answer me. What do you want?"

He slightly lifted his knee off my back and I gratefully filled my aching lungs. It was several seconds before I could speak.

"I thought you would have sex with me," I said.

He shoved against my back again. "What do you want?"

"Sex. With you."

"You want me to fuck you. Is that right? Then say it. Say, 'I want you to fuck me.' Exactly like that."

God help me, I said it, exactly like that.

He reached into the black bag that laid half-spilled nearby. He pulled out a long, purple velvet sack that I paid little mind to earlier. He loosened the tie at the top, then shook out the biggest dildo I'd ever seen.

It was flesh-colored latex, easily over 12 inches long, and thick, too thick. One end was the usual shape of a circumcised penis. But it was the other end that scared me. Sticking out of the other end was a handle.

The Businessman flipped open the tube of lube and squirted a large quantity down the length of the ugly thing. Then he grabbed it by the handle, reached back and shoved it between my legs. He paused for a moment at the entry of my pussy and caught my eye in the mirror.

He tone was fearsome. "Spread your legs."

I didn't. I was going to, or I thought I might, but I was scared, and I didn't spread my legs, at least not fast enough.

It didn't matter, ultimately. He pushed the huge dildo inside me all the same. I gasped at the intrusion of the huge rod of latex. I was clenched tight, afraid. It hurt when he pushed it farther inside me, my tensed muscles no barrier to his invasion.

"Spread your legs."

I obeyed, quickly this time.

He pulled the dildo out of me, then pressed it back in. I cried out. It was too big. How did he not realize that? I felt like I couldn't stretch enough. I couldn't even be sure how much of the thing was inside me. What if there were more to it, more he had yet to shove inside me? No, I thought, please, no more.

It looked brutal, in the mirror, the way he held the handle of the thing, the way it disappeared behind my leg when he shoved the dildo into me. Again. Again. So hard. Too hard. Even as my muscles stretched to receive it, I thought it could not be enough. It was too big. Too much. I grunted and whimpered and twisted.

His knee in my back kept me struggling for every deep breath. My wrists began to ache from the pressure of his hold.

"This is what you wanted," he said.

And he pushed the dildo into me. "You wanted me to fuck you."

He pulled out the dildo, all the way, then stuffed it inside me again. "This is what you wanted."

I began crying, tears running over my nose and soaking into the white linens. My response was a weak "No."

"No what?" Relentless.

"No, no, it's not what I want."

"Then what did you want?"

"You. I wanted you in me. Not that thing. Your cock."

He tossed the dildo aside. I hardly had time to feel the relief of the dildo's removal before he reached into the black bag again. He pulled out a length of cord and tied my wrists together. Then he climbed off of me and flipped me onto my back. My tied hands remained trapped underneath me, the softness of the mattress making the position more bearable than it would have been on a harder surface. I feared what he was about to do.

He climbed off the bed and grabbed my ankles, pulling me toward him, stopping when my butt rested against the edge of the mattress. He dropped my legs and reached for his belt, which he quickly unbuckled, then he unbuttoned his pants and pushed them down along with his underwear.

I only saw his cock for the briefest instant when he paused to rip open a condom package and roll the sheath down his shaft. My tears blurred everything around me. He reached under my knees and lifted them high, spreading my legs as wide as they would go out to my sides, pressing them back toward the mattress.

And then, he began to fuck me. His cock slid inside me and I gasped, not because it hurt or because I was afraid. I gasped because it was perfect. After the big, ugly dildo, he was silky, hard perfection. He filled me, and a bit beyond. I gratefully welcomed his warm flesh after the invasion of cold, inanimate plastic.

He held my legs behind my knees, and he pumped, out and in and out and in.

He said nothing, his gaze on my breasts and pussy, his dick sliding in and out of me. He fucked me with a steady pace which set the entire lower half of my body into a tingling buzz.

He brought my knees back together, then pushed them to one side, my torso twisting with the movement, my ass turning into view, the pressure of my weight gone from one of my restrained arms.

Then he fucked me like that, with my legs pressed together and off to one side. Both of his hands were on my topmost thigh, and his thumbs dug in near my pussy and pulled up, opening me wider. My tears dried and I moaned and tried to grind against him, a practically impossible task in my position.

I kept thinking, "Oh, I didn't know." I didn't know sex could feel like that. Never. Never had it felt like that. Almost overwhelming, the totality of the sensations.

He thrust faster and harder, then landed a fearsome swat on the topmost cheek of my ass. I cried out in surprise more than pain. He grabbed my shoulder, shoving me completely onto my side, never once missing a stroke as he fucked me.

With my whole ass available and vulnerable now, he landed a stinging swat on my other cheek. I cried out, even as he struck again, and again, and again. He smacked my ass until it burned.

He fucked and spanked. Spanked and fucked. And my cries grew louder and he felt so damned good in me that I didn't want it to stop, even though tears threatened a return.

I don't know when the pain of the spanking began adding to the pleasure. I moaned, gasped, made uncountable guttural sounds and didn't give a damn about it. Just don't stop. Don't stop.

He flipped me onto my back again, and spread my legs wide. He left them splayed open, pressing down on my lower stomach with one hand, and using the other to pinch and toy with my clit.

My ass burned. He never stopped fucking me, a constant source of boggling pleasure. Something about his hand pushing on my stomach added a pressure, an urgency. I moaned and moved my hips in rhythm with his thrusts. He rolled my clitoris between his fingers.

And like that, the force that had been building inside, reached its peak and exploded outward. I came.

I gasped and shook, tremors passing through me, the release eclipsing the climax I'd given myself earlier. The Businessman maintained his steady pace while I thrashed underneath him and shuddered and moaned. All thought ceased, and I became a creature of pure sensation, no distractions, no questions, no thought. Only bright and brilliant pleasure.

When the sensations finally died away, my ability to think returned. I looked to The Businessman.

He pulled out of me, his cock still standing out from his body, as hard and long as when I first glimpsed it through the blur of tears.

"Was that what you wanted? What you earned?" he asked.

I answered quietly. "Yes ... no."

He glanced significantly at the big fleshy dildo that lay nearby.

"No, no more. Not that."

He stared at me. I knew that he waited for me to tell him what was missing. I said nothing, though. He bent over and began pulling up his pants.

My stomach flip-flopped. "You," I said quickly. "You didn't come."

He hitched his pants over his hips, rolled off the empty condom and somehow tucked his huge erection away before he buttoned and zipped his pants.

He was buckling his belt when he asked, "You wanted me to come?"

I sat up. "Yes, of course, I wanted —"

I didn't finish because he leaned into me. I flinched, but he only reached behind me and, with a few deft motions, untied my hands. Then he turned and walked away, heading into the bathroom.

I sat there, listening to him running water in the sink. Time moved slowly while I waited. What next?

He was drying his hands on a towel when he returned to the bedroom. I thought he was going to leave, but he stopped and looked at me, his features closed. "What you've failed to understand this evening, though I thought I made the point adequately, is that none of this is about what you want. Needs are a different matter, and since yours have been met, you have no reason to complain."

He picked up his jacket and tie. His voice was appallingly calm. "This is about me, about what I want and what I don't want. That's all it will ever be."

Then he turned and left the room.

I sat stock still. I felt like I'd been slapped across the face. Humiliation boiled up from my stomach and burned in my throat.

I thought of how I must have looked, tossing my head and wriggling my hips, coming and moaning and ... I didn't want to think about it. I didn't want to think about how he'd been in complete control of his body the entire while and I never noticed. I realized now that he hadn't even been breathing hard, or not as hard as I was, anyway.

I'd been punished after all, but not for failing to follow his commands. He punished me for thinking I deserved something from him. Him. It was all about what he wanted.

No. That wasn't it at all. It was worse than that. I truly had failed to understand, precisely as he said.

This wasn't a tryst, or an assignation. I thought I was meeting a sexy man in a hotel room and we'd have a great time together, the way we did in the hallway at the bar. If it went well, and we enjoyed ourselves, maybe we'd do it again.

But I was wrong. Completely wrong. This wasn't an assignation. This was an interview.

I remembered thinking of interviews after he grilled me with those questions in the sitting room, but I hadn't imagined that's what this actually was.

He asked me here to interview me for ... something, I didn't know what, exactly, but that didn't matter so much as the fact that I missed his entire point of our meeting.

I practically begged him for sex, and for him, this was only an interview, an examination, a study of my fitness for whatever task he had in mind for me.

I didn't know how I missed it. He basically told me as much. But I'd missed it.

The memory of me asking him to have sex with me, to fuck me, it wouldn't let me be. I wanted to curl into a ball and never see him again.

The skin on my face felt tight. My throat was dry and my head ached. I didn't want to think about any of this anymore. I wanted him to leave, to go to that other appointment of his, and let me slink away once he was gone.

That wouldn't happen, though. So I walked on shaky legs to the bathroom and got a drink of water. It soothed my throat, but my head still pounded. I splashed my face, washed the dried tears from my cheeks.

I sat on the toilet for a while, trying not to think, but failing. I was pointlessly putting off the inevitable. I would have to see him again. His previous command that I not take too long while I tidied myself, still stood. He had another engagement. No more time to waste on the likes of me.

I winced at my own bitterness.

I got up, wrapped myself in the other bathrobe that hung in the bathroom and tucked my feet into the smallest pair of slippers that sat in a line on the floor. Time to face him.

In the sitting room, The Businessman stood by the bar, knocking off the last of an amber liquid from a tumbler. He thumped the glass down then glared at it as if it were to be blamed for thumping.

Apparel-wise, he was immaculately attired again, jacket donned, tie re-tied. He, unlike me, looked no worse for the wear. He was manly and sexy; I was tired and plain.

He glanced at me, then up at the clock on the wall. "I apologize that I have to leave so soon. I planned to have dinner with you, but my appointment is unavoidable. Are you okay?"

I nodded, headed to the sofa and sank into the soft cushions, welcome on my sore rear. Let this be over soon, I thought.

"You're not hurt, are you?" he asked.

I shook my head. Not hurt, if you didn't count my pride.

"Good. I'm glad you're okay."

I stared at my hands and waited.

"I left my card on the table. It's my private cell number. I've decided I'd like to see you again."

I wasn't sure what to feel. I couldn't imagine why he wanted to see me again. I failed the interview. Impossible to think otherwise. Besides, now that I understood things better, I wasn't sure that I wanted to see him again.

I wasn't exactly angry at him. He hadn't lied to me or hurt me too badly. He had, in fact, given me the mind-blowing orgasm of my life. But that didn't factor into my feelings, not at that moment.

I said nothing, just leaned down and picked up the card. In simple black lettering it read, "Gibson Reeves," and underneath that, a phone number. There was nothing else on the card.

Gibson. His name was Gibson. Finally, a name.

"Call that number," Gibson said, "if you decide you wish to continue our association. We can discuss then what I have in mind for us. Understand that if you do call, you can't also accept Weston's offer."

He didn't wait for a response. "I've got to go. Don't feel like you have to hurry away. The suite is yours for the night. They have an excellent restaurant here, as I'm sure you know. Order whatever you want and they'll charge it to the room. Don't worry about the mess in the bedroom, or putting anything away. The staff will take care of it."

He stepped up to me, leaned down and kissed me gently on the lips. I returned his kiss, because it was expected of me. He tasted like bourbon.

He stroked a thumb down my cheek. "Nonnie, I realize it seemed harsh in there, and I didn't actually intend to ... never mind. That's not important. Just know that I think you're beautiful, and sexy. You please me in many, many ways."

"Good night," he said, and he headed to the door.

I'd been idly turning his card around while he spoke and I noticed a handwritten scrawl on the back of the card. It was familiar to me, identical to the scrawl on the bottom of the note I found when I arrived.

Gibson was opening the door when I asked, "What is this? On the back of the card. I can't read it."

"Oh, of course. It's my name, or rather, the only name for me that you'll need, should you decide to call. It's Sir. For you, my name is Sir."

And he left the suite.

I stared at the back of the card. I recognized the word in the bump and slash of the pen strokes. Sir. Yes, it was there if you looked hard enough, and already knew what it was.

I felt like I'd been in the hotel for ages. How long had it been, really? I checked the clock. Not much past eight. Little more than an hour since he arrived. It didn't seem possible.

I spent the rest of the evening trying not to think. I showered then soaked in the bathtub, adding the scented oils I found tucked away in one of the vanity's drawers, undoubtedly the toiletries the hotel usually offered guests, not the plain unmarked ones Gibson left for me. I washed my hair with the hotel shampoo. It smelled of citrus and cleanliness and I needed the smell of clean in particular.

I fixed my hair, put on some makeup, mainly just mascara, the way I usually wore it. When I was digging in my purse for the mascara, I found The Businessman's, well, Gibson's, tie. I'd planned to return it to him. Nothing to be done about it now.

Regardless of what Gibson told me about the staff, I tidied up the bedroom and washed the latex toys, then returned them to the black bag. I wanted them out of my sight. Put away.

I ordered an expensive meal and ate it on the balcony, wrapped in my bathrobe, comfortable in the cool night air. The lights of the city streets stretched to the dark horizon.

When I finished eating, I got dressed then returned to the sitting room. On a whim, I opened my wallet and took out Michael's card. I laid it next to Gibson's on the coffee table.

So strange, those two rectangles of paper. Odd enough that I was expected to choose between two men. But the cards were strange in and of themselves. They seemed formal and old-fashioned in this age of cell phones and texting. They could have simply input their names and numbers into my phone. Instead, they handed out cards.

Michael's card was of a good thick stock, pure white, with black print. The only adornments were a border of shiny gold, and a barely visible watermark, MW, his initials.

Gibson's card was also of a good heavy stock, also with black print, but the color of the paper was a creamy off-white. There were no adornments of any kind. Even the font was plain.

I stared at the table. Two different cards. Two very different men.

Two offers.

I couldn't have them both, Gibson said. I had to choose.

The Playboy or The Businessman.

One or the other.

Maybe neither.

I scooped up the cards and dropped them into my purse. It was time to go home.

« Chapter 9 »

FOR MORE THAN A WEEK I debated my decision. At work, when I should have been thinking about hiring new temps for the accounting department, I daydreamed about Michael and the sting of his belt striking my ass. When I should have been contributing to a discussion about limiting office waste, I remembered Gibson's eyes on me while I masturbated in front of the mirror. Not exactly thoughts conducive to career advancement.

When I drove, when I shopped, when I cooked, when I showered ... there wasn't a time which wasn't interrupted by a memory of Michael or Gibson, and by speculation about what might happen in the future. How far would I go?

Michael wanted five nights, five opportunities to explore the sensuality he and The Businessman had introduced me to. Beyond those five nights, who knew? My instinct counseled that Michael didn't commit himself to anything for long.

Could the same be said of Gibson? I didn't even know what he was offering. He only said he wanted to see me again, and this was after he thoroughly humiliated me with his interview. Whenever I thought of that night, my skin grew hot all over again and I longed for an escape from the memory of my mistake. Horrible.

Part of me hated Gibson Reeves. The rest of me remembered what it felt like when he was inside me, so the hate got smothered under the memory of his perfect assault.

Michael or Gibson? I couldn't walk away from them both. As much as they unnerved me, they also fascinated and tempted me, luring me further into titillating and forbidden territory. It was impossible not to pursue their lead.

Eventually, I decided I needed a second opinion. Since I couldn't speak with any of my usual friends, what with not wanting to permanently scandalize them, I considered calling one of the two women I recently met, Lilly Smith and Elaine Hoyte.

I wasn't sure how far into the BDSM scene Lilly actually was. It was likely that she hadn't been totally honest with me the night we met. I believed that she had pretended to know less than she actually did, hoping that I would accompany her to Private Residence. I didn't think she had any sinister motives, just that she thought a fib was her best chance to convince me to go with her.

So, chances were good that Lilly knew more about BDSM than I did. I suspected she knew something about Michael as well.

Elaine definitely knew Michael, had been kind to me, and appeared to know a great deal about BDSM. From what I saw of her and her husband, they were pros, if there were such a thing as professionals in sex play, which I doubted even as the notion amused me.

I took a chance and called her. I thought it might be awkward at first, reminding her who I was, and so forth. However, she quickly put me at ease.

"Nonnie? Of course I remember you. The cute little thing Michael was so mean to." The way she said this, though, made it clear that being mean wasn't so terrible a thing.

I couldn't help but smile. "That would be me."

"You still mad at him?"

"I don't know."

She chuckled. "It's hard staying mad at such a sexy guy. I oughta know. It's that way with me and Ron."

I had no idea how good-looking Ron might or might not be, what with the hideous hood covering his entire head when I saw him. It struck me how bizarre that was, and the surprise of it nearly made me end the call right there.

"I saw Michael a few nights ago, and he mentioned you," Elaine said.

"I hope you kept my secret."

"Your what? Oh, that one-way mirror business. Of course I did, honey. Anyway, he told Ron and me that he made you an offer, and you haven't called him yet."

"I'm not sure what I want to do. That's why I called you."

"Sure, sure. I getcha. Michael's pretty hot and bothered about you. Looked put out that you haven't called. He's not used to bein' put on hold." Her laugh was a delightful trill.

"I wasn't trying to get revenge for what he did, but if he's put out by me, it serves him right."

Elaine laughed harder.

"What I called for," I said, "was to ask you out for coffee, or drinks, whatever you want. I have a lot of questions and I don't have anyone to talk to. You were nice to me and it's probably an imposition, but —"

"Now don't you worry about that. I told you to call me, didn't I? I'm real happy to help any way I can."

I sent thanks out into the ether for kind women everywhere. Elaine and I decided to meet the next evening after work at a quiet lounge she said was near her home. She prodded me a few more times about Michael, then we said our goodbyes and ended the call.

I considered what she said about Michael. He was thinking about me. I couldn't deny that I was flattered. I wanted to know more, and Elaine appeared to be the one to tell me.

But there was an obvious place I hadn't yet looked for information, a place I'd been avoiding because I wasn't sure what I was going to do. It was time to search the web. I booted up my laptop.

I found a handful of Michael Westons in the city, and not much information on any of them. After some digging, I thought I found the right one. If I was correct, Michael was the owner of a company called Spotlight Productions, which appeared to be involved in media somehow; it wasn't clear.

The company's web site claimed to offer a variety of media services, whatever that meant. I assumed it meant advertising, promotions, that sort of thing. Mostly, the site was visually flashy but vague in content, using phrases like "capitalizing peak exposure" and "maximum imprint value." Sounded like so much hipster-biz-speak to me, but what did I know?

As for his personal life, his name appeared in several articles about local events, such as a charitable ball that he attended and a wedding where he served as a groomsman. They were all several years old. Older still, he was mentioned as a survivor in the obituary of Lyle Weston, which if my identification was correct, would mean that Michael's father had been deceased for about seven years.

And that was pretty much everything. It didn't tell me much.

If information about Michael was thin, then information about Gibson Reeves was virtually nonexistent.

I only found two mentions of a Gibson Reeves associated with the city. If this was the correct Gibson Reeves, then he was a board member of a privately-held corporation called Roundtree Holdings. There wasn't much information about Roundtree, either. It appeared to be involved with acquisitions and mergers. How large it was, I couldn't say, since it didn't release financials. Its headquarters were in the city.

The only other mention of Gibson was in relation to a six-year-old article in the newspaper about a local nursing home. Roundtree Holdings had purchased the business and the residents were upset that it would be closed and torn down to make room for new development. Gibson was interviewed in the article and had only one quote in the piece, stating that Roundtree had no plans to close the facility.

The article insinuated that there were further fears that the level of care in the home would deteriorate under its new ownership. From what I could see of the pictures accompanying the article, it didn't appear that the upkeep of the place could get much worse. It looked in shoddy shape, with peeling walls and open fixtures.

And that was the sum of information about Gibson Reeves. Or at least, that was all I could find.

I wished I were more savvy about Internet searches. At least I was reassured that neither of them were dangerous convicts, unless their records had been expunged. No point in thinking in that direction.

I closed my laptop and went to the kitchen. I stuck a frozen dinner in the microwave and while I waited for it to heat up, I considered what this lack of information might mean.

When I took into account the nature of both men's sexual predilections, it made sense that they would be private types. I believed that what went on between consenting adults was their own personal business, but I knew plenty of people whose opinions differed.

This knowledge kept me from talking to my friends about what had been going on in my life of late. I didn't know for certain that they would disagree with what I'd done, or with what I was debating doing, but I didn't want to take the chance of losing friendships over something which might not become a permanent part of my life.

Secrets are strange things. I didn't like them, other than the surprise birthday party sort. Secrets implied shame and guilt, wrongdoing. I wanted to be done with shame and guilt.

I wondered about my friends. If I told them about Gibson and me in the hallway of the bar that night, what would they say? If I left out the part where Gibson tied my hands to the light fixture, and how he spanked the hell out of me ... what then? What would they say? I'm sure they would laugh and tease and call me a bad girl, but they wouldn't be serious about the bad part. They'd say good for you, have some fun.

But what if I didn't censor the story, told them everything? I didn't know. However, I was positive that if I told them about what happened with Michael at Private Residence, they would think I'd lost my mind.

Forget, also, any conversation about my second meeting with Gibson. I thought of describing how Gibson tied me up and fucked me with a massive dildo. In my mental movie of my telling the tale, I watched my friends keel sideways out of their chairs, thudding to the floor in a catatonic state.

Okay, maybe that was a bit of a stretch, but there was no way to know what they might think. Not for certain. I couldn't risk it. So I had a secret. Did that mean I must feel ashamed, too?

The microwave timer beeped. I ate in the living room, on the couch in front of the television, my usual routine. I was halfway through dinner and a sitcom when it hit me. Tomorrow evening I would see Elaine Hoyte, and she would tell me more about Michael. A thrill of excitement shot through me.

I wasn't standing still anymore. I was moving forward. To hell with what others might think. Tomorrow couldn't come fast enough.

❧

Elaine was waiting for me when I arrived at the lounge. It was one of those throwback places that hadn't been remodeled in decades. It looked today like it looked in the 1970s. And the recorded music playing softly in the background hadn't changed either; I was fairly certain that the singer was Jim Croce.

Though the place was shabby, it was generally clean. The lighting was low, so I could have been wrong about the cleanliness. I chose to believe I was right.

Elaine noticed my scrutiny. After we greeted one another and I sat down, she said, "Hope you don't mind me choosing this old place. I love it. Makes me feel young because it reminds me of the past. Doesn't hurt that it still smells like cigarette smoke. I quit forever ago, but I miss it to this day."

I assured her I didn't mind and she waved over a waitress to take my drink order. It was different seeing Elaine in street clothes, her brown hair pinned back in a neat twist, her green blouse conservatively buttoned all the way to the top. She looked like any other attractive, white-collar female you might pass on the street, a total departure from the amply-cleavaged, leather-corseted woman I met at Private Residence.

Elaine wasted no time and got straight to the heart of the matter. "So, you've got me here. What do you most want to know? We'll start there."

"Okay, what do you know about Michael Weston? How long have you known him?"

"Ron and I have known him for maybe a year. Met him at a friend's party. He gave an exhibition on flogging. Had this gorgeous gal with red hair all trussed up and, well anyway, you don't want to hear about that part."

"That's probably the part I should definitely hear about, whether I want to or not."

"Well, honey, he's a handsome, single Dom, so he makes tracks. There's usually some woman or other ready to spend some dungeon time with him. I've seen him with lots of different ladies in the past year. He wasn't serious about any of them, as far as I know."

"Does he make the same offer to the women he, uh, dates? Dates doesn't seem like the right word. The women he does his thing with?"

Elaine chuckled. "Does his thing. Close enough. As to your question, I can't say. What did he offer you?"

"Five nights, a five-night commitment to explore whether or not I'm really into the BDSM thing, into being a sub, whatever."

Elaine's eyebrows lifted. "You don't say? Interesting. I've never heard of him doing that before, but don't read too much into it. It's for sure, though, like I said last night, he definitely wants to see you again. Looked like he has it pretty bad. Don't remember him being that way before with anyone else."

That was reassuring. "Do you know if he's ever been serious with anyone?"

"Nobody since I've known him. But really, honey, there's no point in being worried about the future and all. You don't hardly know him yet, so how do you know if you'll even want to see him after your five nights are up?"

Good point. "This is all so strange. I don't know how to move around in this world. I'm not even sure what questions I should be asking."

The waitress delivered my drink then left us alone.

"There ya go," Elaine said. "You're smart enough to realize you don't know a damned thing. If it was me, I'd want to know if Michael has ever seriously hurt anyone, without permission, or went too far and ignored safe words."

I sipped my drink and gave her an "and?" look.

"And the answer is no. I've never heard of Michael doing that. As far as I know, he obeys the rules of safe, sane and consensual. Those are important rules for us in the life. Whatever you do, you want to play with people who obey 'em. Safe, sane and consensual. Don't forget 'em. They pretty much speak for themselves."

"Here's the thing," she said, "I don't want to scare you, honey, but you've got to be careful. Just like everywhere else, there are good and bad people in the life, and it's not easy to tell who's who. We rely on each other to police ourselves. If we learn someone isn't who they should be, we try to make sure everybody else knows about it. It's hard to protect everyone, but we try. And lots of us especially try to protect newcomers like you."

"I appreciate it."

She waved me off. "It's nothing but what we should do. Anyway, that's all just my long-winded way of saying I've never heard about Michael breaking the big three rules. I will say, though, I heard one rumor that bothered me a little."

"What was it?"

"It supposedly happened before Ron and I moved to town. We've only been here about a year and a half, ya know. So, I heard that there was a sub of his spreading it around that Michael hadn't treated her right. The person who told me the story didn't know exactly what it was that Michael did to the gal. It's hard to judge what's true when you've got so little to go by. There's good and bad Doms, sure, but there's also good and bad subs. She could have been lying, wanting revenge for him dumping her, or whatever, or she could have been telling the truth. Who knows?"

"All I can tell you for sure," she said, "is that I've never personally seen him do anything bad to anyone, or at least, not do anything bad that someone didn't give him the go-ahead to do. But we don't spend a ton of time with him, so take that with a grain of salt."

I recalled The Businessman, Gibson, and how he warned me to be careful around Michael. He said I should protect my interests. Maybe he'd heard the rumor, too, and that was why he wasn't more specific with his warning. All the same, it was reassuring that Elaine knew no personal ill of Michael.

"Do you know a man named Gibson Reeves?" I asked.

"I don't know him personally. But I know who you're talking about. People have pointed him out to me."

"Do you know anything about him?"

"Nope. Just hearsay." She studied me. "How do you know Gibson Reeves?"

I debated my answer, not sure how much I wanted her to know. "About who he is, practically nothing. But physically, yeah, I know him. He, uh, he made me an offer, too, sort of."

Elaine let loose a loud peal of laughter. "Well now, Miss Nonnie Crawford, aren't you somethin'? Hee hee! I love you young gals. I tell you what, if I were 15 years younger, and single, I'd be doin' the exact same thing. Two offers, you say? From men like Michael Weston and Gibson Reeves? That's somethin'. Good for you!"

I didn't know what to say to this hearty response. I gave a bit of a sheepish shrug. "I didn't plan it. It just sort of happened. Really. I'm not kidding."

She wouldn't stop chuckling. I shook my head and waited for her to knock it off.

"Oh, I'm sorry," she said. "It's not that I don't believe you, it's just that I had this idea of who you are, and knowing you've also spent time with Gibson Reeves, well, it threw me. It's great. Good on ya. Now listen ..."

She leaned across the table and with a lowered voice, confided in me. "Like I said, I don't personally know Reeves, but I've heard plenty about him. Everybody says he's some super-wealthy big shot, but he doesn't flash his money around the way some rich folks do. They say he's super private and that you never see him in the display rooms at the clubs. Some say they've seen him in action at parties. I doubt it, though. Lots of folks say he's cold and proud, but I've also heard people say he's helped others out of scrapes."

She shrugged. "I even heard a rumor that he's a part owner of Private Residence. I've also heard that he's part of a crime family, you know, like the mob, but I think that's total nonsense. I've seen thugs in my time, and that man's no thug. I'd place a bet on it."

"Also," she said, "I've never heard anything about him not obeying the rules of safe, sane and consensual. Not even a hint of it. Nothin'. Some of these women make it sound like they'd trade their first born to have a chance to be with him. Don't give me that face. Okay, maybe I'm exaggerating a bit on that one, but still."

So, my Gibson was a source of rampant conjecture for the local BDSM community. I wasn't surprised. My experience with him proved how enigmatic he could be. Also, I was now certain that Michael hadn't been truthful about his knowledge of Gibson. If Elaine had heard all these rumors, then certainly Michael would have. Perhaps Michael didn't want to spread gossip.

Elaine interrupted my speculations. "So what kind of offer did he make you? Come on, girl. Give it up."

I smiled at her. "Honestly, I'm not sure. He wants to see me again, that's all I know."

Elaine made a singsong sound like, hmm-hmm-hmm-hmm. "This is what I call a serious dilemma. I don't suppose there's any way you could have both of them, is there?"

I enjoyed how she lightened the situation. I laughed. "Afraid not. I was told I have to choose."

"Well, damn! If that isn't just like Doms for ya. Oh sure, they wanna share and all, but they still demand a main claim to their sub. Wouldn't wanna be in your shoes tryin' to pick between those two. Oh, hell, who am I kidding? I'd love to be in your shoes."

"I don't know, Elaine. I feel like I've been trying to figure this out for ages."

"That's okay. We'll work it out. We can make pro and con lists for both of 'em."

I couldn't help but smile at the absurd suggestion. The idea of making a pro and con list for choosing a dominant — ridiculous. "Let's not," I said.

"You're right! I have a better idea. Now just hear me out."

"Okay."

"The way I see it is this. You've got two hot men interested in you. They've both got a lot to recommend them. Both have money. If the rumors are to be believed, Reeves has a big edge on that one, but I know that Michael's set financially. He owns some kind of media business. What else? They're both good Doms as far as we know. They're both good lookin' in different ways."

"Yeah, you've already said they're hot."

"Indulge me, honey. I can't help myself. Anyway, like I said, they're hot in different ways. Reeves has that dark, mysterious action, and Michael's got those wolf eyes and that long hair."

"Ha! You think they're wolf eyes, too."

"Don't know what else you'd call 'em. Let's see. What else. Oh, Michael's younger, closer to your age. How old are you? Twenty-five, twenty-six?"

"Twenty-nine."

"Michael's only a few years older than you, then. But Reeves must be closer to 40, around my age. That's a pretty big difference."

Gibson didn't seem old when he was fucking me, I thought, but kept that part to myself, not wanting Elaine to expire of apoplexy.

"Age isn't really an issue for me," I said.

"Al-righty then." She pursed her lips and thought for a moment. She squinted at me and a slow smile spread across her face. "We agree that it's pretty equal between them, right?"

I told her yes.

"Then here's my idea. I know you're supposed to choose just one and all. But I guess I'm not seeing why you can't have your cake and eat it too, if you know what I mean."

"I have no idea what you mean."

"You're not thinking rationally. You said you aren't even sure what Reeves is offering. But you know that Michael is asking for five nights."

I nodded. Wow, this woman did enjoy drawing things out.

She wasn't done yet. "So what's to stop you from accepting Michael's offer of five nights? Give him the full tryout. Then, when those five nights are over, you'll give Reeves a call and take him up on his offer. You see what I'm saying?"

I had to admit, I was beginning to see it, and I liked the way she thought. "But Gibson said I had to choose, that I can't have them both."

"Oh honey, it's just five nights. Reeves probably meant a permanent choice of some kind. Don't look at me like that. For all you know that's what he meant. Anyway, what are the chances he'll find out you accepted Michael's offer first?"

Hmm. The woman had a serious point. She was tempting me, and she knew it.

"Come on now," she said. "It's the perfect solution. And anyway, you might find out that you don't want to be with anyone but Michael after those five nights. Who's to say? I just think you shouldn't burn your bridges with Reeves. Accept Michael's offer, but don't tell Reeves that you did it. Nothing wrong with that."

"You're a wily woman, Elaine Hoyte."

She grinned. "Don't I know it. Come on. Do it for all us old gals who'll never have a chance at something like this."

"Right, I'll do it for you 'old gals.' You don't seem old to me."

"I'm old enough to tell you not to pass up a chance like this. I've got age and wisdom on my side. I'm just sayin'."

"I think you're convincing me."

"Good for you, honey." She raised her glass.

I took a long drink and considered Elaine's argument. Why not do it? Who was Gibson to order me to choose anyway? I was a modern woman living in the twenty-first century in a free country. I mean, sure, this BDSM stuff had medieval elements about it, but I personally wasn't living in the Iron Age.

For the first time since I'd been put in the position of choosing, I felt pretty damned good. I didn't have to choose. Elaine was right. I could have them both, if I wanted.

I was going to do it.

I called the waitress over and ordered another round for me and my devilish mentor.

Elaine and I chatted for nearly another hour. She grew serious at one point and began talking about some of the things I should know about BDSM. Before I left, she gave me a list of Web sites she recommended to newbies and told me to get out there and educate myself.

Back in my apartment, I ate a quick dinner and tried to pluck up the courage to call Michael. I noticed Gibson's tie hanging over the back of a chair. How many times had I looked at that tie during the days since I last saw its owner? How many times had I held it to my nose, remembering how it felt to kiss him, to have his hands on me? To have him inside me.

All of this started with Gibson, with that tie. I picked it up, took it to my bedroom, draped it over a hanger then hung it up at the very back of my closet.

Gibson may have begun this journey, but I'd be traveling the next stage with Michael. I returned to the living room and found my cell phone.

As soon as I placed the call to Michael, my nerves kicked in. What if he didn't answer? What if I had to leave a message?

What would I say? Hi, you wanted to have five dates with me. No, that was stupid. Hi, I want those five nights you offered. Better, but not good enough.

Turned out my practice message was of no use. Michael answered on the second ring. "Hello?"

"Uh," was my sterling response. "Yeah, Michael. This is Nonnie ... Nonnie Crawford. We met the other night at —"

"Nonnie," he said, his voice as smooth and sexy as I remembered, "finally, you called. I was beginning to give up hope. I thought I might have to hunt you down and convince you in person."

"You're assuming that I'm calling to accept your offer."

"I'd never assume anything with you. I'm simply pleased to hear your voice. I'll admit, though, I'm hoping you've called to tell me yes. I've thought about you many times since we met."

"I've thought about you, too." Duh. Understatement.

"If you think it might help, I'd be happy to meet with you tonight. Try to persuade you."

"I'm aware of how persuasive you are."

His low laugh sent a shiver through me.

I spoke quickly. "But that won't be necessary. I want to say yes to your offer, but I need to clarify a few things first."

"Wonderful. Anything you want. Just ask."

"Okay, you said five nights to explore these new feelings."

"Yes, to explore your submissive side."

"Right. Well, what would that involve? I mean, I'm not sure about —"

"You don't need to worry about what we'll be doing. I'll make those decisions. I can assure you it will be extremely sexual. Extremely. I've thought about doing all sorts of wicked things to you."

He paused for a moment. "I'll be your guide and I'll do my best not to push you further than you're willing to go. But you can always say no. If I do my job right, you won't need to."

"I don't know how this works, though."

"That's what part of the time will be for. I'll tell you what you need to know, when you need to know it. It's my responsibility to guide you, and I take it seriously. Trust me, Nonnie. You won't regret it."

I shivered again. No, I couldn't imagine regretting time spent with Michael. Well, as long as I didn't break some stupid rule.

"Okay then," I said. "Yes, let's do this. I'm ready."

"I'm pleased. I wish I could drive to your place and start tonight. But, unfortunately, there's some business we have to attend to first."

He asked me a few things about my sexual history, similar to the questions Gibson had asked me, though less detailed and fewer in number. He wanted my email address and said he would sometimes use email if he had special instructions for me, or needed some information.

Lastly, we arranged to be tested for STDs and agreed to share the results with each other. It was this detail that would keep us apart for several more days, since Michael preferred to wait for the results so we could be confident when we were together.

"I'll be thinking of you," he said before we hung up, his words loaded with that heady combination of desire and danger.

I told him I'd think of him, too. I meant what I said. The next several days would pass slowly.

I had done it. A rush of excitement filled me.

He had said, "I've thought about doing all sorts of wicked things to you."

Five nights with Michael, doing ... extremely sexual things. But what, exactly? I craved to know.

One thing I knew for certain, had learned the lesson the hard way from Gibson Reeves in that hotel room: whatever Michael and I did, it would be what Michael wanted it to be.

I savored the anticipation of it. The rousing flashes of fear.

He would take and I would give.

Whatever The Playboy wanted.

EXCERPT FROM

The
PLAYBOY'S
Proposition

The Power to Please ❧ Book Two

« Chapter 1 »

I WANTED TO BE SWEPT away in a grand and passionate love affair. I wanted it to wrap itself around me and raise me out of the monotony I had made of my life, of myself. I needed that perfect love to vindicate my past.

My past was an embarrassing cliche. Raised by parents who lost interest in me around the time I began to form my own opinions of the world, I sought reassurance of my worth from others. When I discovered the appeal of my youthful sexuality, I believed men could provide that worth.

It wasn't long before I discovered how mistaken I was in that belief. By the age of eighteen, I was pregnant. I thought my boyfriend was more than gallant when he proposed marriage, and it made me love him. When I miscarried the baby not long after our wedding, I stayed with my new husband.

Not that I had much choice, really. My parents had kicked me out when they learned I was pregnant, attacking me with accusations and character affronts which assured I wouldn't speak to them for years. I was on my own. No money, a high school diploma, and a husband who believed he would be a rock star one day.

I learned how to survive, took shitty jobs that barely kept a roof over our heads and food in our mouths. And because I needed to believe that I could have a better future, I took night classes at the local community college.

By the second year of my marriage, I learned why my husband actually married me. It hadn't been for the sake of our baby, or to provide for us; it had been because he wanted someone to take care of him.

I remember him storming around our one-room apartment, berating me for not making enough money for him and his band to go on the road. It was all my fault, he said. All my fault because I hadn't listened to him, hadn't done what needed to be done.

He wanted me to give up night school and become a stripper. Better money, he said. I didn't need school, he insisted, because he would be a star soon, and you didn't need a college degree to be the wife of a rich rock star. All I had to do was to sacrifice for him now, and I would be repaid later.

I was actually proud of myself for telling him no, that I wanted to stay in school, that I would stay in school no matter how much he yelled at me. I told him to get a day job to make the money to go on the road. He kicked the furniture and stomped out of the apartment. I didn't see him for a week.

I find it hard to accept, now, that I was proud of telling him no. I'm disgusted with my past self that I allowed him back into my life, let him stumble back into my bed, drunk and stinking after a week on the streets doing God knew what. I should have thrown his ass out the door.

I could say no to his demand that I become a stripper. I couldn't say no to the marriage.

So many wasted years, supporting a man I loathed, and who loathed me in return in spite of my efforts to appease him. Not his fault, though. My fault. I knew the truth by year two of my marriage. That it took me eight more years to finally unload him … well, that was on me.

I desperately needed to shake the blame for those ten years of bad decisions and lost chances. I longed to banish the taint of my failed marriage, of failed dreams.

I was now twenty-nine years old. I had a college degree, a decent job, a place of my own, and a sense of urgency to claim a different destiny. Divorcing my husband was only the first step. I needed something more than a job and an apartment. I needed what I had never had.

A great love, a great passion. That was what I wanted. To float away in undeniable desire. Love could do that for me. And if not love, then passion alone could surely do, for now.

Two men offered me passion, Michael Weston and Gibson Reeves. Michael, tall and lean with the charm of a continental playboy. Gibson, who I still thought of as The Businessman, tall and muscular, with a handsome but inscrutable face.

Both of them, dominant males who saw something in me I hadn't known was there. A sexual submissive, driven to be taken by their power. Me, into BDSM. Were they right about me? I didn't know, for certain, but I wanted them to help me find out, was more than excited by the prospect of their special assistance.

Michael proposed five nights to explore my newly-discovered kink, and I had accepted. As for Gibson, I wasn't certain what, precisely, he might have planned for me. After the fiasco of my "interview" at the Frederick Hotel, he simply said he wanted to see me again. For one night only? More than that? I didn't know. But if things didn't work out with Michael, it was likely I would be calling Gibson to find out exactly what he had in mind.

For now, my immediate future passion lay with Michael. And oh, how I anticipated seeing him again, although I had no idea what to expect. All I knew was that Michael would be making the rules.

My job would be to please him, to see if by pleasing him, I pleased myself. I did not take my job description lightly. I swore to myself that I would do my best.

We had completed our agreement to take mutual STD tests, and now were waiting for the results. The wait was excruciating. Time passed in slow motion.

I attribute this to the phenomenon of time passing normally until you decide there is something you want to do. At that point, the universe conspires to slow the rotation of the Earth, the solar system and the Milky Way itself, resulting in a few days of normal time stretching into the length of a month. Stephen Hawking has probably written something about this. If he hasn't, he should.

I slept poorly, often awakened by sexy dreams starring Michael and sometimes Gibson. This might not have been a bad thing if I could have stayed asleep all the way through the grand finale of my dream. But no, every time I was getting ready to orgasm, I would wake up. It was frustrating beyond belief, and possibly another result of the universe conspiring against me.

Finally, after an age, our test results came in; we were both clean. I would see Michael that night.

I received an e-mail from him telling me to be ready at 7:30 that evening. He didn't say what we would be doing, only told me to dress casually.

At precisely 7:30, he knocked on my door.

I took a last look around my apartment. Everything was tidy, though the place wasn't much to look at. I had lived here for over nine months, but I never seemed to find the time or inclination to decorate. There was little in the apartment beyond the basic utilitarian needs of furniture to sit on and a bed to sleep in.

When I left my ex-husband, I didn't take many belongings with me. I wanted to leave everything behind me, and I pretty much did exactly that with the exception of some old photos, my clothes and shoes, and general necessities like toiletries. Everything else could be replaced with something new, something not contaminated by my old life.

I rented the second apartment I viewed. I would have rented the first one I looked at if I hadn't seen a cockroach in the kitchen. My current place was clean, free of bugs, had a new paint job, and was in my price range. Sold.

It wasn't a large place, with only one bedroom, a small bathroom, and a large open-room design that was a combination living room, dining room and kitchen. As I glanced around the living room, I noted how bland it all was. I wished I had spent some time and money on it, put something into it that would show something about me.

My heart beat quickly when I opened the door to Michael. He looked wonderful, even better than I remembered. His shiny black hair was pushed behind his ears and curled at the ends right above his shoulders. He wore a blue silky shirt and a tight pair of faded jeans. He smelled of musk and the outdoors.

He was tall and made my apartment seem smaller than normal.

He smiled at me and said hello. He held my hands and kissed me gently on the lips. I kissed him back, a little shyly, then gestured him into the room and shut the door behind him. I squirmed a bit when he looked around the room, but he made no comment on the place.

He said, "You look beautiful."

"Thanks. You look great, too."

He frowned. "It won't do, you know."

"What won't do?" I asked.

"The pants you're wearing. They're forbidden, I'm afraid."

"Do you have a grudge against pants? I thought these were pretty nice ones."

He tsk-tsked me, then said, "Right out of the gate and you've already broken a big rule. I was afraid, after our first time, that you might be a difficult one. You'll have to be punished, of course."

"That's not fair. You never told me not to wear pants. Anyway, you're wearing jeans, so what's the big deal?"

He chuckled, and said, "I'm teasing you. I just thought you looked pale, and now there's some color in your cheeks."

"I think you like keeping me off-footed."

"Off-footed. I've never heard that one."

"I may have just made it up."

"Then I must be making you nervous."

I thought, nervous maybe, but most likely, you're making me brain dead, which is what happened to me the last time I was with you.

I changed the subject and asked, "Would you like a drink?"

"No, thank you. Those pants actually are going to have to go, you know. From here on out, you don't wear pants when you're with me, unless I specifically tell you to."

To think that I had been worried he might be critical of my apartment, when he only had eyes for my apparel. I said, a tad snippy, "Okay, I guess. I can change into a skirt if you'd like that better."

Two minutes and he'd already annoyed me. It was difficult to stay annoyed, though, seeing the sexy way he was looking at me.

He said, "One idea I'd like you to become accustomed to is that all your holes belong to me, and I should be able to access them as easily as possible. Pants make access difficult, therefore, no pants."

"My holes," I said.

"Exactly. Your mouth, your pussy, your asshole. They're all mine."

I wondered how long it would be before I wasn't surprised by his bluntness. It was something of a struggle to keep up.

I said, "I see. What about my nose and ears? Those have holes."

"Those are mine, too, but I'm not likely to fuck them."

"Ugh."

"Your disgust doesn't bother me. In fact, it kind of turns me on."

"What about my breasts? They aren't holes, so are they mine?"

"Oh no," he said, passing a wolfish gaze over my chest. "Those are definitely mine, too."

"Do any of my body parts still belong to me? How about my wrist? I'm kind of partial to it."

He took me by the arm and raised my wrist for a light kiss. "Never. It's mine. Everything is mine."

Tingles spread up my arm from where his lips touched my skin. "Funny. I don't remember putting myself up for sale."

"Scandalous! You aren't for sale. You've given yourself to me, and I've happily accepted." He looked into my eyes. "By agreeing to be my sub, you're allowing me to do as I please with your lovely person. Yes, I know, there are limits, and I'll respect yours as they come up. But still, you're all mine."

Michael's light blue eyes seemed to darken when he spoke of owning me. I couldn't look away. I said, "I suppose we should talk about those limits."

"There'll be time for that later. Right now, I want you to take off those pants."

"Right now? Right here?"

"Yes, right now. Take them off."

"You're just saying that to get me off-footed again."

He said, "Not true. I really want you to take your pants off."

"It's kind of sudden, don't you think? I mean, you just got here and all."

"Maybe it's a test."

A test. Of my obedience? I had sworn to myself, going into this thing, that I would approach the situation seriously and honestly, that I wouldn't back away from anything that wasn't truly dire. This wasn't dire. Far from it. In fact, his command had unloosed more than a few zippy twinges down low in my belly.

I took a deep breath and, savoring a moment of feeling super daring, slipped off my shoes and pulled off my pants, tossing the pants onto a nearby chair.

Michael approached me then reached between my legs and slipped his fingers under my panties and into my slit. His fingers were warm and electric on my flesh. Gulp.

His fingers slid easily into my folds and I realized I was already damp. I wasn't surprised by it. I had been in a half-state of arousal ever since I told him I wanted to see him again.

Michael smiled and removed his hand. He said, "I had a certain plan in mind for us this evening. But now that I'm here, I think an adjustment might be required."

He continued, "You say this is sudden, but to me, I feel like it's been forever. All I've wanted to do since the moment I met you was fuck you senseless. Besides, I don't want to risk you breaking the rules and ruining everything again. Guess I'm going to have to fuck you right now."

My heart gave a loud thud in my chest.

He began unbuttoning my shirt. "I seem to recall you wanting me to fuck you."

I winced at him recalling the embarrassing way our first time together had ended. Please, I thought, don't piss me off now. Or worse, humiliate me.

He tossed my shirt on the chair, then he turned me around and undid the fastenings on my bra. He said, "I've thought of that so many times since I last saw you. And I've regretted that I couldn't grant your wish."

He slipped my bra off my shoulders then sent it flying away to lie with my other clothes. He turned me back around to face him, then tugged my panties down to my knees. In a few seconds, I was standing naked before him. I shivered, but not from cold.

"I love your body," he said. Then he removed his shirt.

I was pretty fond of his body, too, and reached out to touch his sculpted chest. He pushed my hand away.

"No, you don't touch unless I tell you to," he said. He kicked off his shoes and socks, then removed his jeans and underwear. "You have to earn that privilege."

We stood there, looking at one another, naked. His cock stood out stiff and proud. My breath grew ragged, and I noticed Michael's, too, was getting harsher.

"Tell me again," he said, "that you want me to fuck you."

"I want you to fuck me." And I definitely meant it.

"Call me Master," he demanded. "Say, I want you to fuck me, please, Master."

This was more difficult for me. Calling him Master was not something I felt wholly comfortable doing. Still, I had done my reading, and knew Master was a common honorific.

I took a deep breath and said, "I want you to fuck me, please, Master," as smoothly as I could. It wasn't as awkward to say as I had feared.

He said, "When we're in private, you will address me as Master, unless I tell you otherwise."

I nodded.

He said, "Say, yes, Master."

I did.

He made a low sound that revealed his pleasure. He said, "Now come here and put your arms around my neck and kiss me."

This was an easy order to obey. He wrapped his arms around my waist, pulled me tight against his chest and returned my kiss. He tasted minty and clean, and I savored the pleasure of his tongue pushing into my mouth, the force of him claiming this particular hole. His hole, he had called it. I shivered in his arms.

His hands roamed over my back and ass while he deepened our kisses. I slipped my fingers into his hair, glad finally to get the chance to feel the texture and weight of it.

We kissed and explored some more, then his hands gripped me under my ass and he lifted me up, telling me to wrap my legs around his waist. His erection pressed against my stomach as he carried me to the sofa and sat down. I unwrapped my legs before he leaned back, leaving me straddling his lap.

He pulled my hips toward him, grinding me against his hard dick that was trapped between our bodies.

He said, "Put your hands on your head, lock your fingers together like that. Yes. Now, ask me to suck your tits. Say, please suck my tits, Master."

I grabbed some air and managed to say, "Please, suck my ... tits, Master."

"Say it again, like you mean it."

"Please, suck my tits, Master."

"Gladly, sweet one," and he leaned forward and sucked one of my nipples into his mouth.

I panted and melted into the sensations of his hot mouth on my breasts and his hands gripping my hips, pushing and pulling me against his engorged cock, and me joining in the rhythm of the grind, my wetness smoothing the ride.

Michael nibbled at my breasts and nipples. Tiny little bites, soft love bites. In between nibbles, he asked, "Do you like that?"

I moaned out a yes.

He bit down harder then said, "Yes what."

I gasped. "Yes ... Master."

He murmured, then continued suckling and nibbling my breasts. I closed my eyes and rode him.

When he finally pulled away from me, he told me to put my hands on his shoulders for balance, then he had me rise up onto my feet into a crouched position over his lap. He held his dick and had me lower my body until the head of his cock was pressed against my opening. He told me to hold the position.

It was not an easy thing to do. I was trying to hold a low squat, my knees spread wide to either side. I had a tight grip on his shoulders, and within a minute my thigh muscles were beginning to ache from the pressure of crouching. But the worst of it was having his dick right there, teasing me. I wanted him inside me.

Michael, meanwhile, was eyeing my pussy. I could not have been more open to his view. He pinched and pulled at my labia.

My legs began to quiver. He said, "Keep holding it. I love seeing you like this. You're all wet and slick, and ready for me, but you can't have it, not quite yet."

He pulled and pinched and pulled. I moaned. He smiled and licked his lips. He said, "Tell me you want my dick."

I panted and answered, "Yes, I want your dick."

"No," he said.

I quickly responded, "Yes, I want your dick, please, Master."

"How do you want it?"

"I want it inside me, Master ... please."

"No, say it filthy and raw, and real."

I said, "Please, Master. I want your dick in my pussy."

"Whose pussy is it? You're forgetting what's what."

"Okay. Yes. Right. Please, Master, I want your dick in my hole. I mean your hole. Fuck me, Master."

He growled and ran a thumb over my clit. I fought to hold my position with my quivering legs.

He gave me one last sharp pinch then said, "Lower yourself, Sweet. Slowly."

I did. I felt myself stretch to take in the size of him, the hard width and length. I groaned.

He said, "Take it all. All the way. Yes, like that."

I could feel the head of his penis pushing deeply into me, all the way down to the hilt. He filled me and then some.

"Move your hips in little circles," he said.

I did. Mmm, so good. So good having him inside me. Then he had me rise up again, back into my former position, and he had me hold it for a few moments while he played with me, then I was allowed to lower myself back down again and circle my hips. Then up again. Hold. Then down. And circle. Up. Hold. Down. Circle.

Every time he flicked my clit I was in danger of coming. He warned me not to orgasm, ordering me to wait until he told me to come. I hadn't expected anything different. But it was hard. It was hard to take in all these sensations, to feel the heat and pressure growing in my lower belly, and know I couldn't release it. So hard.

He said, "I love seeing my dick slide into you. Your pussy spreading open to take it all. Tell me you want to please me."

"I do," I managed to say between my gasps. "I do want to please you, Master."

"Good. Then take it all. Yes. Now switch to your knees ... like that, yes. Hands back on your head. Arch your back. Perfect. Look at those tits. You have beautiful tits. Stick them out for me. Ahh, yes."

His hands closed around my waist and he lifted me then shoved me back down hard. I gasped. Again. I made a mmph sound.

"Up and down hard," he ordered. "I want to see those tits shake. Up and down. Hard! Fuck your master's dick. That's right."

I rode him as hard as I could, needing his assistance at my waist for additional force and balance. His hips jerked under me and rose up to meet me when I pushed down onto him. His eyes watched my bouncing breasts, and my pussy, and a few times, my face.

I panted for breath while the pressure began to grow unbearable. Finally, with one of his hands, he rubbed my clit. Catching my eye, he said, "You can come now."

I worked my hips and tightened my muscles, feeling the force of my impending orgasm begin to flow outward. Pure pleasure washed over me and I cried out, throwing back my head and shutting my eyes then ...

Pain. Harsh pain on my breast. I cried out and jerked backwards, trying to yank away from the pain. I looked down. Michael was biting my right breast. His mouth was open wide, clamped down over nipple and areola. His lips were pulled back and I could see his white teeth sunk into my flesh, not breaking the skin, but pressed deep. Deep enough to hurt. To hurt badly.

I cried out, "No!" The pain blended with the pleasure of my orgasm, pleasure that hadn't stopped just because I hurt. Pain and pleasure, both at the same time.

Michael released me, pulling back and looking sharply into my eyes. He saw my pain and smiled a wicked smile that only grew wider when I covered my aching breast with my hands. He clamped down hard on my waist, pounding me up and down on his cock. He held my gaze and fucked me.

Then he came. The last of my orgasm faded as his semen spurted into me. He groaned, and drew heavy breaths as he finished. And all the while, he never looked away from me.

I was still holding my breast, a bit in shock, I think, from what had happened. Michael pulled my hands away and when he leaned his head toward me, I pulled back, thinking he was going to bite me again. He laughed and pulled me forward, stretched out his tongue and licked my breast.

He licked me and suckled and soothed the ache away. Because of the intensity of the pain, I expected to see deep indented teeth marks on my breast, but there wasn't much of a mark at all, just a circle of reddened flesh.

His hands skimmed over my back and down my hips. I began to calm down.

At last, I said, "I don't understand why you did that. Why you bit me."

He smiled and gave a little shrug. "I did it because I wanted to. Was it that terrible for you?"

"Yes, it was. It scared me."

"Nothing wrong with a little fear, Sweet. It heightens the passion."

"And it hurt. I don't like that."

"Are you sure?"

"Yeah I'm sure. What kind of question is that?"

He said, "Don't you think maybe the pleasure is greater with a bit of pain thrown in for an extra boost?"

"No, I don't."

He laughed. "You just came like a freight train and you're telling me it wasn't pleasurable ... you are completely charming."

"I didn't say it wasn't pleasurable. I meant I don't need pain for pleasure. Unlike you, I guess."

"Oh, I don't need to be in pain to get pleasure. I don't see how you've gotten that idea."

"That's not what I meant. I meant that you need me to be in pain for you to get pleasure."

"That's ridiculous. Not true at all. Yes, your pain is something of a boost for me, but I don't have to have it. I just want it when I want it. Don't look like that. You can't blame me for it. You're spectacular when you're in pain, did you know that? Spectacular. And fear, ahh. Your pretty brown eyes, they grow even bigger and wider when you're afraid and in pain. Lovely. So lovely."

He stroked a thumb down my cheek with his last words. I hardly knew what to think. He pulled me down toward him and nuzzled my neck. His breath warmed my skin when he said, "It wasn't so bad, really, was it?"

I made a noncommittal sound.

One of his hands gently cupped the breast he had bitten. His fingers played lightly over my nipple. He said, "The pain is already gone. It was nothing after all. You were more surprised than anything else."

I mumbled a maybe. It was hard to think when he was doing these things to my body. His kisses on my neck, one hand on my breast, the other stroking my hip. A tendril of heat curled in my belly. I wanted to know more about his need to hurt me, I had questions ... I just couldn't remember what those questions were anymore.

Michael said, "You're already getting excited again, ready for more, aren't you? Don't be embarrassed. I think it's wonderful. I think you're wonderful. I'd like to take you again, right now. Can't you feel my cock getting hard again, already?"

Yes, oh yes I certainly could.

He said, "I swear I had plans for us this evening. If we don't get up now, I'll have to fuck you again. Come on. Let's get up. We've got things to do."

He lifted me off of his lap and set me down beside him on the sofa. He immediately got up and looked around my apartment.

"Where's your shower? We'll clean up, get dressed and be off. What do you say?"

I tried to shake myself out of the passion stupor he had put me in and said, "Okay."

I led him back to my bathroom.

Things didn't go quite as he planned there, either. It wasn't a quick shower at all. Perhaps if we had showered separately ... oh well. Slick and wet bodies aren't exactly deterrents to sexual arousal. I was given free rein to explore his taut body, the planes of his flat stomach, the curve of his hard ass. I guessed I must have earned the right to touch him, and it made me happy, actually did feel like something of a reward.

He eventually pushed me against the shower wall and took me from behind, all slow and silky and sweet, his hands on my belly and breasts, mine on his tight buttocks. No pain this time. Just the pleasure. Our orgasms, like the warm water, streamed over our bodies.

So it wasn't a quick process, the cleaning up and the drying off and the getting dressed again. He picked out a skirt for me, which he had me wear without any panties underneath, and a shirt, which he wanted me to wear without a bra under it. I felt dressed and naked all at once.

Then we were outside, in his dark blue sports car, tearing down the streets of the city, headed I didn't know where. I didn't much care. I laughed easily at the teasing things he said, and I enjoyed my quick heartbeats whenever he slid a hand up my thigh and under my skirt, teasing me in this other way.

I felt beautiful and free and alive ... and young, younger than I had felt in years. This was youth, riding in a fast car with a powerful and handsome man who wanted me, and who I wanted in return. At least, it's what youth should be. It was what every day should be.

He asked if I was hungry, but since I wasn't, he said we would go straight to the mystery location he had planned for our first date, though date wasn't really the right word for what we were doing, was it?

I half-noticed the passing buildings becoming shoddier, the neighborhoods becoming poorer. Soon, I realized we were in one of the more dangerous parts of the city. I asked Michael where we were going, but he only smiled and said I would find out soon.

He pulled into the parking lot of a garishly-lit building, all neon and flashing lights. A strip club? No. Close, though. It was an adult book store, in other words, a porn shop. And not a nice one. It was tacky and sleazy, and didn't look altogether savory.

I said, "You know, there are a couple of places like this in better parts of town. Places where I wouldn't be afraid of catching a disease from touching the front door."

Michael laughed. "Those antiseptic places? There's no fun in that."

I frowned. "They use antiseptics for a reason, you know."

He laughed again. "You're perfect. Just perfect. Come on. Let's go in."

"I'm not going in there. It's probably not safe."

"Safe from what? Who do you think is in there? A bunch of gangsters?"

"I don't know. Maybe."

"Let's go find out."

I eyed the place, looking around the parking lot to see if I could spot anyone coming and going. There were a handful of cars in the parking lot, but no one out walking around. "Seriously," I said, "I don't want to go in there."

Michael lost his smile. "Seriously, I want you to go in there. With me. I'll protect you. Trust me."

I looked into his eyes. He wanted this from me. I felt that if I argued any further, I'd be somehow implying that I didn't believe he could protect me. I didn't want him to think that. But still. I sighed.

I said, "Okay, I'll go in. But I'm not touching anything."

He regained his smile. "No problem. I'll do all the touching," he said, and squeezed my knee before he opened his door.

I was self-conscious when he helped me out of the car, thanks to my panty-less state and the inherent difficulties of getting out of small sports cars. This was insane. Going into a place like this with no panties and no bra and who knew what kind of people inside.

True to his word, Michael held the door open for me when we reached the building. I walked inside the tawdry place and took a look around.

« CHAPTER 2 »

WE WERE IN A LARGE room, well-lit, with lots of shelves holding merchandise like books, movies, magazines and sex toys. It smelled like plastic, and paper, and unwashed men.

There was a counter near the door where a grizzled elderly man sat perched on a stool, looking bored as he watched a small television that sat near the cash register. He glanced at us momentarily then returned to watching TV. I would have thought seeing a woman in here would be a novelty for him. Apparently not.

Michael said in a low voice, "Don't make eye contact with him or he might turn violent. You know what they say about animals like him."

"Funny," I said.

He chuckled, picked up a shopping basket by the door, then put his free hand on the small of my back and steered me down one of the aisles. He asked, "Have you ever been in a place like this?"

I glanced at the plastic-encased covers of the magazines we were passing. Big boobs everywhere. Really big boobs. Giant boobs. What the hell was wrong with men, anyway?

I said, "Once, when I was younger. Some friends and I went to one of the nicer adult places in the city."

He stopped and inspected the cover of a magazine that catered to lovers of big butts. "What did you think about it?"

"We laughed a lot. I think the saleslady wanted to kick us out."

"Probably so," he said. "What do you think about all these magazines here? Hundreds of them. Look at all the different kinks."

"I see. Have you got a thing for big butts? I notice you're seriously checking out 'Asses Aplenty' there."

He shrugged, "It depends. Right now, I've only got eyes for your cute little ass, my sweet."

He steered me on down the aisle to a group of fetish magazines, including a range of BDSM offerings. He pulled a few off the shelf and dropped them into the shopping basket.

I didn't get the chance to see what he had taken so I asked, "What are you buying?"

"A couple of personal favorites. They're for you. For research, later."

"Oh," I answered stupidly.

"In fact," he said as he led me out of the magazines and into the DVD section, "this whole excursion is meant to be a shopping trip just for you. How fun, right?"

"Uh, I guess."

"I've never seen a woman who was unhappy to have things bought for her."

"That's sexist. And anyway, I'm pretty suspicious of your motives here."

"Don't be ridiculous. My motives are obvious."

I said, "Not to me."

Michael's pale blue eyes sparkled. "I want to thoroughly corrupt you so I can do all sorts of filthy unspeakable things to your delectable person. I really did think that was obvious."

Oh my. I gulped, but recovered quickly and whispered, "Keep your voice down. Please. I think that nasty perv over there heard you."

I shot a glance at a middle-aged man standing not too far away. He appeared to be something of a derelict and I didn't like the way he was looking at me.

Michael just shrugged then led me on past the gawking man, and into another aisle, this one full of sex toys.

Michael said, "I want you to pick out a toy that you'd like me to use on you. Go ahead, look around. Anything you'd like."

Okay, I thought, this might be doable. I looked at a slender rod-shaped latex toy with a flat end. The label said it was a butt plug. I said, "Well, I don't know for sure what this is for, but from the name, I'm thinking it's not something I'd like."

"Pity." Michael sighed. "It's beginner size. Let's take it anyway, just in case." He snatched it off the shelf and dropped it in the basket.

"Put that back," I hissed. "I do not want my butt plugged, whatever the hell that means."

"You don't know what you want," Michael said. "Keep looking."

I surveyed the shelves, glancing right past some gargantuan-sized butt plugs, the massive double-headed dildos and the open-mouthed blow-up dolls. Oh hell no.

I didn't comment when Michael picked up several items and dropped them into the basket. He grabbed up three dildos of different sizes and textures as well as a handheld vibrator.

I studied a very small vibrator. It was only about the length of my index finger and about twice as wide around.

I said, "I guess you could use this on me."

Michael snorted, tossed it in the basket and said, "I was getting that anyway. Pick again."

This was hard. I didn't know what half of the stuff was for, and the other half, I felt pretty sure I wasn't up to trying. I soon found myself at the rear corner of the building, rapidly running out of options to select from.

I faced the loaded shelves and felt helpless. How ridiculous, I thought. I wondered if I started giggling loudly would the old man at the counter throw me out of the place? Rescued by an attack of the giggles. Perfect.

Michael stepped behind me, set the basket on the floor beside us, and slipped his arms around my waist. I snuggled back against him.

He said, "Your brow is all furrowed up, you know. You look like you're having to choose an implement of torture."

I sneaked a glimpse at the nearby row of whips and handcuffs and riding crops. "Oh God. Don't make me do that."

He snorted. "I would never buy a torture device here. Those things over there are shoddy play toys. We have real shops for the serious tools. This place is just for fun."

I only managed an mmm-hmm.

He squeezed me. "You're a difficult person to understand, Nonnie Crawford. In the club last week and back in your apartment, you were different than you are right now. While I could see your inexperience, you were willing to try new things, broaden your views. And now in this place, you're acting uptight and scared. You won't even choose an item meant for your pleasure."

"I don't know why I'm acting like this," I admitted.

"You should relax. There's nothing scary here, not the customers, not the merchandise. Take a few deep breaths and relax."

I breathed while he slowly ran his hands up and down my arms, a soothing touch I hadn't realized I needed.

He said, "Look at that package there, the one with the two silver balls connected by a cord."

I found the package. It was one of the items I had noticed but didn't know what it was supposed to be used for, or what it might do. The balls were about an inch and a half in diameter.

Michael continued, "Those are called Ben Wa balls. They're supposed to have originally come from China, and have been used for centuries."

He rubbed across my belly and over my hips. He said, "The balls are hollow, with another smaller ball inside. They're meant for pleasure. Pick up the package. Feel the weight of them."

I did as he asked. They were heavier than I thought they would be. When I gently shook the package, I could feel the smaller balls rolling around inside the larger ones.

Michael whispered close to my ear. "Imagine your legs spread wide and me pushing those balls into you." His fingers played with the fabric of my skirt. I could feel him lifting the material slightly.

He whispered, "I'd have to oil them up pretty heavily because they're so big. You'd have to stretch to take them in. I can see your pussy lips widening as I push one of the balls inside you."

His words were beginning to affect me, but not so much that I didn't notice him slowly lifting my skirt. I nudged one of his hands, wanting him to stop.

He said, "Shh," and ignoring my hand, lifted my skirt higher. "Close your eyes and give in to the moment, Nonnie. There's no one back here and they couldn't see anyway because I'm behind you. Give in, sweet. Let me show you what you're meant to feel."

I breathed deeply and tried to do as he asked. I wanted to feel. I wanted to be different. I wanted to be led ... didn't I? I closed my eyes.

I knew the moment Michael had pulled my skirt up enough to fully expose me, felt the open air on my skin. His fingers played over my upper thighs and teased around the edges of my pussy. His hot breath sounded in my ear.

He took the package of Ben Wa balls and dropped it into the basket on the floor, then said, "I want you to hold up your skirt for me."

I took a shaky breath and reached for the bunched up fabric he had been holding. I fought my natural impulses to make him stop. Give in, I told myself. Do as he asks. I clenched my skirt in my fisted palms.

"Good," he said. Then his hands found my breasts and he cupped them in his hands and squeezed them firmly. "Oh, yes. This is how I want you. So open. Everything here for me. You don't know how much this excites me, knowing it's hard for you and that you're doing it anyway ... for me."

He lightly pinched my nipples under the silky fabric of my shirt. I squelched a moan. He said, "This next thing I want will be harder, but you must do it, do you understand?"

I nodded. He exhaled harshly. I quickly said, "Yes, Master, I understand."

He kissed my ear then said, "You can drop the skirt in front, but I want you to lift your skirt up over your ass. I want your bare ass up against my jeans. Do it now. Don't think, just do it." And he pinched my nipples harder with those last words.

And somehow, I did it. I bared my ass right there in that store.

"Beautiful. Perfect," he said. He slipped a hand between us and kneaded one of my ass cheeks. "You're wonderful," he said, and I practically purred from the praise.

I arched my back and pushed my ass harder against his groin. I tried to control my rising need while I basked in this small moment of surrender, of overcoming my feelings about this place, about what he wanted of me, about what I wanted of myself.

I let everything go while he fondled me, stroked me, pinched and aroused me.

Eventually he said in a husky voice, "Open your eyes and look back to your left."

On autopilot, I did as he asked. I think my heart stopped beating for a moment at what I saw. It was the pervy man I had seen earlier. He was watching us, watching me. I immediately stiffened.

Michael quickly said, "Don't think. Remember. Don't think. Now look to your right."

I did as he asked. Another two men were watching us, two seedy-looking men watching me with Michael.

I tried to pull down my skirt but Michael held my hands and said, "No, let them watch a few more minutes."

I hissed, "No. I'm done here. I can't do it." I fought to get my skirt down.

Michael said, "You can do it. Because I want you to. Because deep down, you want to."

"No! You told me I could say no and that you'd stop. I want you to stop, now."

He released me. I dropped the hem of my skirt, then turned and glared at the three gawking men until they finally took my not-so-subtle hint that they'd best clear the hell out, the show was over. All the while, Michael stood there casually watching me, studying me, maybe.

I smoothed my clothes and tried to control my breathing. I said as calmly as I could, "If we're done here, I'd like to go now."

"As you wish," Michael said, and picked up the basket.

We didn't speak while he ushered me up to the front of the building. I looked straight ahead, avoiding any eye contact with the other customers. In my opinion, we couldn't get out of there fast enough.

The old man at the counter took ages to ring up all of Michael's items, his gnarled old hands shaking from palsy, taking multiple stabs at entering the prices into the cash register. The man didn't look like he could fight off a small child, let alone a dangerous hooligan, and I had to admit that Michael was undoubtedly right about there not being much of a safety issue in the place.

Finally, on the third try, the old man managed to complete the sale and Michael and I headed to the car. And then we were driving away from the sordid site. I exhaled in relief.

Michael asked me if I was hungry now, but I again told him no, that I hadn't even thought of food. He simply said okay, then didn't speak again. All the fun and pleasure of our ride to the porn shop was gone.

I snuck the occasional glance at him while he drove. His handsome face was impassive. He didn't appear angry, or even annoyed. In fact, he looked pleasant enough. All the same, the silence bothered me. We were going to have to talk about what happened, weren't we?

I waited quite a long time, hoping he would open the conversation. When this didn't happen, I debated what I might say. I wasn't angry at Michael for what had happened. My reaction had been more panic than anything else. Did he understand that? Should I tell him?

I hated the silence. It seemed to go on forever.

I settled on asking, "Are you mad at me? For stopping it?"

Michael answered simply, "No."

I couldn't read anything into his tone. It was just a no and nothing else. That wasn't telling me anything.

I said, "I just couldn't do it. They were so ... ugh. It was gross."

"What do you mean?"

"I mean, they were nasty. All dirty, and pervy and ... gross."

"Oh," Michael said. "So, if they were nice-looking, clean men, then you wouldn't have minded? You would have kept going as I asked you?"

"Well ... I don't know. No, I don't think I would. I guess I haven't thought about it."

"You should think about it, Sweet. You had no problem displaying yourself at the club the other night. How many people watched me squeeze your breasts? And in the private room, all three of those people saw you completely naked. You gave me a blow job in front of them."

I was glad it was dark in the car so he couldn't see my blush. I said, "That was different."

"How? Because they were all freshly showered?"

It was impossible to miss the sarcasm in his tone. And yet there was no world in which I would tell him that I had thought the glass in that room was a one-way mirror. It was too embarrassing. No chance.

I copped out with, "I don't know. It's just different."

Michael shook his head. "I want you to think about all of this, and try to understand what's keeping you from acting on what I believe is a natural tendency toward exhibitionism."

"I'm not an exhibitionist."

"How do you know?"

I sighed. "I don't know, Michael. It seems like that's all I can ever answer. I don't know."

We rode in silence for a few minutes, then Michael said, "You should understand that it's common in the BDSM community for Doms to show off their subs to others. I'm one of those who enjoys doing it. I think that you're someone who would be aroused by being shown off in public, regardless of what you think yourself."

He continued, "If you wish to please me, then I hope you'll work with me on this. Obviously, I was mistaken about your comfort level, and pushed you too far tonight. I'm prepared to go slower with you, if you're willing to keep an open mind and trust me to guide you."

I thought about what he said. A part of me fought against him characterizing me as someone who didn't know her own mind. It made me think of a man patting a woman on the back and saying, "Don't you worry your pretty little head about it. I'll take care of everything." I bristled at the very thought.

And yet, the way Michael spoke, it didn't sound condescending. He sounded like someone who genuinely believed I was unaware of my deeper desires, and that he could help me discover and accept them. What if he were right?

I remembered being at the club with Michael. Yes, in the club at large, I knew people were watching Michael play with my breasts. It was a heady feeling, all those eyes on me, but I wasn't really showing anything. Then in the private viewing room, I hadn't realized I was being watched. I was embarrassed when I discovered the truth, though most of the embarrassment stemmed from my stupid assumption about the glass.

Then there was my encounter with The Businessman, Gibson Reeves, in the back hall of that bar, something about which Michael knew nothing. I remembered Gibson taunting me with the possibility of someone discovering us back there, and I distinctly recalled how his words excited me.

Maybe Michael was right. Maybe I didn't truly know myself. And maybe it was time I faced up to some uncomfortable truths. He said he would go slow. And so far, he had kept his promises.

I said, "Okay. I'll try to keep an open mind. And I'll trust you, Michael, to guide me, for now."

He smiled, his teeth a flash of white in the dark car. "Good. You've made me happy, Sweet." Then he reached over and squeezed my knee.

I laid my hand over his and smiled. I told myself, you can do this. And I believed I could.

We arrived back at my apartment building not too long afterward. He jogged around and helped me out of the car, and I waited in the entryway while he dug through the bags he had tossed in the trunk.

Once we were in my apartment, Michael kissed me gently on the lips then said it was late and since we both had to work the next day, we should call it a night. He told me he had plans for the next night, but that if I were free the night after that, he'd like us to get together again. I told him that would be fine for me.

Before he left, he handed me a small package. It was the little, pocket-sized vibrator he had purchased for me.

He said, "I want you to use this before you go to bed tonight, at least three times tomorrow and one time the morning after that."

I took the vibrator and said I would do what he wanted.

Michael looked into my eyes and said, "When you use it, think of me, and what I've done with you, and what you might like me to do with you. But most importantly, right before you're ready to come, I want you to think of someone else being there with us, watching us, watching you. When you've done that, you have permission to come. Do you understand?"

I told him I did.

He continued, "It's important that you obey me in this. You're not allowed to come until you fantasize that someone is watching us. If the fantasy keeps you from coming, then so be it, you won't come. Understand?"

"Yes," I said, regretfully.

He said, "One last thing. Stop thinking so much, and worrying over everything. This is supposed to be fun. Sexy and fun. Promise me if you start analyzing, you'll stop yourself, because I've asked you to ... and because it will please me. Say you'll please me and obey me. Say it properly."

I said, "I promise I'll please and obey you, Master."

He said, "Good," then reached a hand behind my neck and pulled me in for a deep, long kiss. I was half breathless by the time he released me.

We said our goodbyes, and too soon I closed the door behind him. I leaned back against the door and stared at the little vibrator in my hand. I had homework. I smiled at the thought. Best homework I'd ever gotten, assuming the intrusion of a third person in my fantasies didn't blow the whole thing.

And I had been ordered to stop worrying, over-thinking. That thought made me smile even more. It was like being given permission to be reckless and wild. Not that I needed a man's permission to be reckless and wild but ... oh no, I was over-thinking again. And I had promised not to do it. Stop it, I chastised myself.

In a few moments, I had stopped. Good for me. Excellent.

And then I realized I was starving. Hungry at last. I headed off to the kitchen.

ৡৡৡ

ABOUT THE AUTHOR

Deena Ward writes erotic fantasies with a classic twist. She believes there could be nothing finer than having a job which demands she spends her days in worlds of her own creation.

She lives in the Midwest USA with her partner and a rowdy, plump beagle.

Visit Deena's website and subscribe to her newsletter to keep up to date on book releases and other important announcements.
http://www.deenaward.com

BOOKS BY DEENA WARD

The Power to Please series:
The Businessman's Tie (Book 1)
The Playboy's Proposition (Book 2)
His Name Is Sir (Book 3)
The Submissive's Last Word (Book 4)

Made in the USA
Middletown, DE
03 October 2017